About the author

Jamal Abozaid is an Arab-world writer and historical fiction novelist and is currently based in London. He writes, lectures and travels extensively. An expert in Arab world issues, Jamal appears on various different media outlets, as a commentator on Middle East politics, imigration and social issues.

STARVE OR KNEEL

Jamal Abozaid

STARVE OR KNEEL

Vanguard Press

A CIP catalogue record for this title is
available from the British Library.

ISBN 978 1 784653 67 5

Vanguard Press is an imprint of
Pegasus Elliot MacKenzie Publishers Ltd.
www.pegasuspublishers.com

First Published in 2018

Vanguard Press
Sheraton House Castle Park
Cambridge England

Printed & Bound in Great Britain

Dedication

For all the victims of al-Assad's regime and those of his allies.

Prologue

Accompanied by the slogan, 'Starve or kneel', around a million Syrian people had been killed by the dictatorial regime, several millions more wounded, and hundreds of thousands arrested. People had come to prefer death over being arrested by the soldiers of the monster of Damascus. Most of those abducted would never be released and would die at the hands of ruthless executioners after unbearable torture. From the time al-Assad's family had come to power, tens of thousands of prisoners had been killed in the darkness of prisons and detention centres. Apart from the killing, millions of homes and buildings had been destroyed completely or partially across the entire country. Russia and Iran had worked alongside the vicious regime to use every means to kill and destroy. There had been deliberate targeting of civilians, with massacre after massacre with the intention to claim as many souls as possible. They had used jet fighters, strategic bombing aircraft, long-range missiles, artillery, chemical weapons, gas and phosphoric bombs as well as barrel bombs.

The regime and its allies had imposed lethal sieges and sanctions on cities and towns that had fallen under control of rebels, resulting in the death of large numbers of people from a lack of medicine and shortage of food and water. In that gloomy atmosphere, more than half of the Syrian population had been displaced. Most had become refugees in neighbouring Turkey, Lebanon or

Jordan. Others had travelled to Western countries for their safety. Many had died attempting to reach European Union countries, the safe place, in unsafe boats and dinghies in sometimes bizarre and horrible circumstances.

It was clear that the international community had become powerless in the face of Russian forces, those of the Syrian regime forces and their allies, including, Iran, Hezbollah and other Shi'ite militias. One could see the results of this clearly in particular in the bombing of Aleppo at the end of 2016. The only thing the United Nation was able to do was to announce that the massacre in Aleppo was genocide and a war crime.

An astonishing complexity of forces ranged against the people of Syria and people came to understand their own resilience in the face of that. Reality became mixed-up with fiction in al-Sham state. Its people, including its intellectuals, became confused and unable to distinguish 'between a date and piece of coal' as the saying goes, in this planned mess. It was a tragedy how a people could be dragged into such chaos and adversity.

The first stage of the atrocity in Syria continued for five years. Searching for reality, under the wreckage of destroyed cities and in rivulets of blood while the haze of bone-black smoke covered the horizon, was like searching for a whisper.

It was a tragic situation with dreadful humanitarian aspects with a sectarian regime and its bloodsucking allies, including, Shi'ite militias and mercenaries from over sixty-five countries, led by Iran and Russia, resolute in their determination to kill ordinary Syrian people under the rubric, 'War on Terror'.

Chapter one

"Kill me, please! Shoot me! I order you to do so." Ali al-Halabi, one of rebel leaders, shouted to a member of the group close to him, the moment he was injured. He was bleeding and in agony.

It had been a fierce fight and the Syrian regime supported by air forces and its troops on the ground, had made significant progress against the insurgents. Bashar al-Assad and his coalition were able to force rebel groups to retreat without being able to take with them comrades who had been killed or wounded. There was destruction in the city and there were lots of casualties on both sides. Ali was badly wounded by shrapnel lodged in his left leg. He threw down his rifle having run out of ammunition and took off his shirt and tightened it around his wound to stop the bleeding. After that, he crawled towards the remains of a destroyed building to take shelter. One of regime's soldiers spotted him.

"There's one of the dogs there!" the soldier yelled.

Ali was surrounded by the regime soldiers. He was brutally kicked, beaten and humiliated until he fell unconscious. He was then taken by military truck to Jami'at al-Zahra Air Forces Intelligence Service, the Mukhabarat Jawiya, in Aleppo.

General Adeeb Salama, the branch director, stared at Ali with anger for a moment without uttering a word then shifted his gaze to one of his officers, "I want this pig alive. I don't want him dead. We need him. Do you understand?"

"Yes sir, understood." The officer replied.

Adeeb frowned adding, "summon a doctor for this idiot."

It was early morning, Jamil Hassan, the Mukhabarat Jawiya Chief, was in his office, at the Air Forces building, in Ameryat al-Tayaran, in Abu Romans district, in Damascus, reading reports, when there was a knock at the door. Major Hider Nizar entered. He saluted the chief.

The chief sighed. "What's up, Major, Hider." he asked with despair.

"Sorry to disturb you, sir." Nizar said with a smile. "We have good news." and he went on, "There's very important information just received from one of our agents. One of the leaders of the rebels has been captured in the north of Aleppo. He's one of the toughest terrorist fighters. He seems to be an important figure amongst the terrorist groups. And now he is in our hands, sir."

"Great," the chief commented. "What's his name?"

"He is known as Abu Najeeb. We still don't have much information about him."

"Where is this dog right now?"

"He is in the Jami'at al-Zahra branch," Nizar said, adding. "He was wounded in the battle at Handarat."

Jamil nodded and smiled, "This is really good news."

The officer smiled back, "I will call the branch to get more information about him and then inform you sir."

"Leave that to me, Nizar." Jamil said, then lit a cigarette and went on. "By the way, what happened to that stubborn prisoner, Majid? How did he die?"

"He was uncompromising. I have never seen people like these bastards, sir. He refused to deal with us in any way. He spat in my face when I came close to him even whilst he was being tortured and he also tried to bite me when I smacked his face. I had to shoot him."

Then he sighed bitterly, "Anyway, we got rid of him, sir. And he has been buried in the mass grave with the other dogs."

"That's fine, Nizar, although I did want him to suffer more," Jamil commented.

"He was stupid and refused to work with us even though we offered him a good chance and tried every way. I was kind and lenient with him. Unfortunately this approach didn't work."

Jamil crushed the cigarette in the ashtray and yelled. "He deserved to be killed. Bastard!"

"By the way, there's also good news, sir, from Handarat. Our guys taught the terrorists a lesson there and killed a large number of them." Major Hider Nizar said.

Jamil picked up the telephone and called the Director of Jami'at al-Zahra branch, General Adeeb Salama.

"Yes?" Adeeb answered.

"This is Chief Jamil Hassan."

"Yes, sir. I am all ears."

"We've heard that you've captured one of the terrorist dogs. Is that correct?"

"Yes, sir, that's right."

"Have you interrogated him?"

13

"Not yet, sir, he was badly wounded and was unconscious. We only know that he is called Abu Najeeb and that he is one of leaders of the Ansar Eddeen group."

There was a moment of silence.

Jamil sighed. "Well, we desperately need him," and went on. "How badly injured is he? Is it life threatening?"

"No, sir. I think he just needs a few days and he will be fine."

"Good," Jamil replied. "Well, I will send Major Hider Nizar to interrogate him at the branch. I want to collect as much information as possible about him and his activities. You must bring his file to me as soon as possible. He may be the key to our plan to destroy the terrorists. I think he has been sent by heaven at precisely the right time. We must do something to please the President. We are desperate for information. Do you understand what I mean?" Jamil added.

"Understood, sir!"

A few hours later, Major Hider Nizar arrived at the Aleppo branch. He was received by the Director of the branch. "Welcome, Major Nizar," Adeeb Salama said.

"Thank you, sir." Nizar nodded, "How is the dog now, sir? Is he able to talk? Can I begin the interrogation?"

"Certainly, Major. That's no problem at all. Use this office and all the branch's facilities to help you with your task but you must bring me all the information you get from the prisoner. You are under my command here. Understood?"

Nizar nodded. "Yes, sir."

Major Nizar called for Abu Najeeb to be brought to the office as soon as Adeeb had left.

Ali was carried into the office by two well-built soldiers. His face was pale, with signs of fatigue and agony, his clothes had been stained with blood and he could hardly walk. The major stared silently at him for a moment. His heart was hammering against his chest. Then he diverted his gaze to the soldiers who were standing firmly and holding the prisoner.

"Leave him and wait outside," he ordered.

He looked back at Abu Najeeb and shouted, "What's your name, you filthy dog?"

"Ali Hussein al-Halabi."

The major paused for a moment, "Which group do you belong to?"

"The Free Army," Ali answered with feeble voice.

Nizar frowned, "The so-called Free Army!" he said, adding, "You're all dogs, animals!"

Then he stood up from his chair and smacked Ali hard across the face and kicked his wounded leg.

"You are all our slaves! We are your lords. And you'll remain so forever, you idiot! You must obey my orders. Understood!" Nizar shouted.

Ali screamed with pain. He lowered his head as a single tear slid down his cheek.

The major smiled. "You were acting like Rambo in the battle, you bastard, but now you are crying like a woman."

The interrogation took several hours. Major Nizar asked Ali hundreds of questions about his background, his activities and his position within the rebel groups structure. As soon as he had finished with him, he called two soldiers and ordered them to put the prisoner in an individual cell. The two bulky, ruthless soldiers pushed Ali into a tiny, filthy cell, which was three storeys underground.

"This is your place, you bastard," one of them spat out.

Ali opened his eyes as wide as he could. It was a dark, smelly cell. He was struck by the disgusting smell of urine, blood and damp. He closed his nose for a while and leaned against the wall, blocking his eyes as he had a sharp pain in his head. Suddenly he heard swearing, screaming, crying and pleading from detainees in other cells. "This is my destiny," he thought. "I don't know why Abu al-Walid didn't shoot me even though he was so close to me when I gave him an order to do so. It is strange that he left me and didn't even try to recover me or give me a hand."

He closed his eyes for relief because his wound was terribly painful. Suddenly, he heard a voice coming from the cell next to him. "Leave her for me, Jafar. There are plenty of women in the centre. You can choose any other one," one of soldiers was saying to his colleague.

There was a moment of laughter followed by a feeble voice of woman pleading, "Fear Allah. Please, don't do that."

It was clear that the man called Jafar was ignoring her pleading. "Okay, Abbas, there's no problem at all, I will leave her for you. Enjoy the night!"

A few minutes later, Ali heard the woman screaming and pleading, "Please leave me alone, please don't touch me. Don't do that, fear Allah, ple —"

Ali blocked his ears with both hands and heart-wrenching tears flowed down his cheeks. "I wish I had died," he said to himself. "What kind of beasts are these people? They're absolutely animals! I would never have imagined that a human being could become heartless and do such evil things."

* * * * *

The Chief of the Mukhabarat Jawiya ordered a Turkish coffee and lit a cigarette. He was in his office reading a file in front of him when he heard a knock at the door. He lifted his head and shifted his gaze towards the door. "Come in!"

General Adeeb Salama saluted. "Sorry to keep you waiting, sir. It was very difficult to cross the terrorists' strongholds. I had to use a civilian car," Adeeb said.

"That's all right, Adeeb."

"Since the terrorists have acquired Tow American anti-tank missiles we were unable to use military vehicles."

"Actually, I haven't much time to spend with you. We will discuss this matter in another meeting because I have a meeting with Mr Ali Mamlouk, the National Intelligence Chief, who has summoned me to his office this afternoon. There are lots of developments in the conflict."

Adeeb nodded. "That's fine, sir." He handed him the interrogation papers and Ali's file. "This is the dog's file, sir."

"Thank you, Adeeb."

Jamil Hassan opened the file and looked at the photos of Ali al-Halabi and his family. Then he began to read the report.

"Ali Hussein al-Halabi was born in Aleppo in 1982 into a poor family. His father worked as a farmer. In 1999 Hussein al-Halabi and his family moved to al-Atarib. Ali graduated from Aleppo University in 2007 as a pharmacist. He didn't find a job in his field after graduating. He worked as a part-time minibus driver. No one in his family was a member of the Ba'ath party. Also nobody in his family was a member of brotherhood or other Islamic groups. Ali became a member of the rebel group or so-called 'Free Army' in 2012. Two years or so later he became a local leader of the Ansar Eddeen group, one of the terrorist groups. He has been married to his cousin, Zineb Omar al-Halabi, for more than five years. He has no children, but his wife is now pregnant after receiving long-term fertility treatment. He has been eagerly awaiting his first baby. He is a family man and has no relationship with any other women. He is very religious. He doesn't smoke and doesn't drink alcohol. He is diehard and resolute. His wife's father is one of the leaders of the terrorist group al-Nusra Front. He, too, is a very dangerous, tough and resolute person. And he is well respected by all the terrorist groups. His brother-in-law, Majid, has been executed under interrogation."

The Chief raised his head up and looked at Adeeb. "This is good." He nodded his head, "I will study it later."

"I know that it is a big file. It will take some time." Adeeb smiled.

Jamil stood up from his armchair and stared at Adeeb. "Anyway, we have a golden opportunity, Adeeb, to get rid of the most important terrorist leaders at once. There is credible intelligence information that a meeting will take place next week in Handarat. Also, there's trusted information that Mohammed al-Julani, the al-Nusra Front leader, will be among them."

Adeeb nodded with astonishment. "Al-Nusra Front's leader? That's a big fish."

"Yes. That's right. We have to make every effort to kill him. You have the National Intelligence Chief's authority to proceed with the operation, and it is all with Mr President's approval."

"I am ready to act, sir. You don't know how much I hate al-Julani, sir," he sighed deeply. "That bastard has killed many of my family and friends," Adeeb said.

"That will be a big success! We will gain the president's pleasure." Jamil sighed and went on, "So, Ali al-Halabi is a trusted figure within the terrorist groups and a well-respected fighter. We need him to work for us. He is the only one who can carry out this mission. We should use the carrot and stick tactics to bring him under our influence."

Jamil Hassan lit a cigarette and had a sip of his Turkish coffee. "By the way. Coffee or tea, Adeeb?"

"Tea, please."

"There's one point I don't understand, sir." Adeeb exclaimed, adding, "Can you explain what Ali al-Halabi's role will be in the operation, sir?"

"He will carry out an assassination. He has to be convinced, by whatever means, to accept the task. Major Hider Nizar is a most vicious officer. I believe he is capable of forcing Ali to work for us. This type of person is not easy to co-opt."

"Major Nizar seems to be ruthless and vicious."

Jamil smiled. "He's clever as well. I trust his abilities and we can rely on him."

Chapter Two

It was a rainy, cold and dull evening in winter and Nadia, a five-year-old girl, suffering from autism, went missing whilst everyone in the camp was taking shelter from the heavy rain. Suad Homsi, Nadia's mother, was running around the camp deranged, her tears flowing down her cheeks, her heart was beating so fast as she looked frantically for her daughter, asking everyone in her path. She was praying, *"May Allah help me to find her."*

"Where's my daughter? Where is she?" she was saying to herself whilst searching her neighbours' tents.

Suad's destiny had brought her with her family to Zaatari Camp, which had opened in July 2012, by the Jordanian government. More than one hundred thousand Syrian refugees came from all across Syria and were gathered in the filthy camp in the most miserable of conditions.

Bashar al-Assad and his allies had turned Syria into a kind of hell. Hundreds of thousands had already been killed and many more had been wounded. Most Syrian cities had been demolished or damaged. Thousands of Syrians had been arrested. The regime's prisons, police stations and intelligence centres were full of detainees. Millions of Syrian people had been displaced, including Suad Homsi. A huge number of them had been forced to leave. In this apocalyptic situation, many of the Syrian refugees who had crossed the border into neighbouring

Turkey, Lebanon and Jordan were women, who had lost their husband, and children who had lost their parents and extended families.

Suad had left her house, family and dreams behind, having been forced to flee the country with her children following the abduction of her husband by Bashar al-Assad's security forces because of his role in the protests against the regime. She had been advised by close relatives to leave the country. The Mukhabarat Jawiya had captured her husband, Mansour Fadil, and would arrest her if they found out that she was sewing the revolutionary flag and helping her husband to distribute them amongst the rebels.

Mostafa Salem, a freelance newspaper reporter, was visiting the camp to document the chaos of the refugees in the camp in winter. He stopped when he saw a little girl playing with her muddy doll in a puddle. He looked at her astonished. She was barefoot, dirty and rain-soaked from head to toe.

"Why don't you go into your tent? It's raining a lot," he asked her with a compassionate smile.

She smiled back at him without answering.

"What's your name, darling?"

She ignored him completely.

"Where's your home? Where's your mum?" he added with surprise.

She looked at him motionlessly then walked away. He followed her. "Where's your tent, darling?" he asked her again.

She didn't reply but was still smiling.

"Who knows this girl? She seems to be lost," he asked a passer-by and nearby tents' residents.

"I don't know," everybody answered.

He took off his coat and covered her because she was trembling with cold. He was very upset as he walked through the muddy pathways of the camp, holding her hand. He couldn't think of a word to say to her. She just kept smiling. Lots of thoughts and questions arose in his mind. *"How shameful! Where is UNESCO? Where is the UN? Where is the UN Security Council? How can the Arab League let down these poor children? They are without food, basic provisions, proper shelter and education. Where are the human rights organisations? Where are the Western governments? All the world should feel ashamed in front of this little girl. They should all feel guilty. She's not a terrorist. She's not an al-Qaeda member. She deserves a better life, like other children."*

He paused for a moment to ask another passer-by. He kept asking people on his way.

Everyone said, "I don't know."

He returned to his thoughts. *"The monster of Damascus would not have been able to kill his people, destroy the country and displace millions if the major powers had been serious in their claim that they wanted to help the Syrian people get rid of him. Why did they give a false signal to Syrians at the beginning of the uprising that Bashar al-Assad had lost his legitimacy and must go? Why didn't the international community intervene to stop this tyrant from killing his people in the same way they had done in Libya with Gaddafi? Instead they turned a blind eye and gave him the nod to deal with the Syrian people in whichever way he wanted. Why?"*

"Nadia!" Suad screamed and ran towards her daughter the moment she saw her. She hugged her and

22

burst into tears and sighed in relief, "Nadia, where were you, darling? I missed you, my love!" then she turned at Mostafa quickly and said, "Thank you so much, sir! I appreciate your help."

"Is she your daughter, madam?" he asked.

She nodded, "Yes sir, she is."

"How old is she?"

"Five."

"It is strange that she hasn't started talking yet? I asked her her name, where her family was, where her tent was, but she never answered me. I was staggered."

"Her name is Nadia," Suad said and paused for a moment to wipe her tears away, "Sadly, she is autistic," she added.

"I am so sorry, madam, I didn't mean to upset you," he said with sadness. Then he nodded his head, embarrassed. "Does she receive any treatment or care here?" he asked.

Suad groaned and wiped away her tears. "No. None. Since we arrived in the camp three months ago, she hasn't had SSRIs or any other medicine."

She sighed from the depth of her heart in great sadness and he handed him his coat. "Anyway, thank you so much again, it's very kind of you, sir. May Allah reward you. Excuse me sir, I have to go. My other children are waiting," she added.

"I am a freelance journalist. Can I arrange to interview you later, madam, to send your voice out to the world? It is very important that the world becomes aware of what is going on in this miserable camp and how you are suffering."

"No, I am so sorry. I still have a family inside the country and my husband is between the jaws of the monster. He is in one of the regime's prisons. I know that if I utter a single word the regime will take revenge against him."

"I promise you that your name will never be mentioned if you agree to an interview."

"I'm afraid with respect, I don't trust the media. They're all liars," she added, whilst walking away. "I don't think anyone in the world doesn't know about our tragedy."

He nodded and asked, thoughtlessly, "By the way, what's your husband name?"

* * * * *

A few hours later, Ali al-Halabi was transferred to another cell, packed with prisoners. He remained standing, gazing at the inmates with astonishment. They were sleeping almost on top of each other. Some of them were practically naked. He wasn't able to count them all as there was very little light. He was struck by the smell of decay, the heavy stink of disease and infected bodies, sweat, urine and blood in the airless cell. He closed his nose and mouth as he was half-faint. His heart-wrenching, his eyes watering and his stomach heaving. *"This is unbelievable. How can this tiny room accommodate so many people?"* he thought.

"You can sit here, brother," one of the prisoners whispered.

Ali squeezed himself in between two of them. "Thank you." He said with grief.

"My name is Mansour Fadil," the prisoner said.

Ali stared at him absentmindedly and remained silent.

"Are you okay?" asked Mansour.

"Yes, I'm fine."

"From which part of Syria do you come from?"

"Al-Atarib."

Mansour nodded, "Al-Atarib! What's your name?"

"Ali al-Halabi."

"You look injured, Ali. Was that the welcoming party?"

"No. It was from fighting in a battle. What's the welcoming party?" Ali asked.

"Anyone who arrives in this branch is welcomed by the soldiers. They kick, beat and torture the prisoners regardless of age."

Ali nodded with sorrow and sadness and said, "I had my share of torture."

"Be patient, brother. Leave everything for Allah. Life and death here are the same," Mansour said nodding and went on, "Get some rest, brother. The torturers can come at any time to take you out for a beating."

Mansour paused for a moment, looking around and whispered. "I advise you, brother, not to trust anyone in the prison. There are some agents among us."

Ali was silent for a moment and thought, "he is right, but, how do I trust him either?"

"By the way, do you know Majid al-Halabi. You've got the same family name," Mansour added.

"He's my cousin, he was also captured, fifteen months ago, and since then we have heard nothing about him."

Mansour wiped his face. His eyes welled with tears.

"Do you know anything about him?" Ali asked, surprised.

"Majid was a hero. I have never seen such a brave man. We were together in the torture chamber. Unfortunately, he died under torture. He didn't comply with the interrogator and he spat in the face of the officer when he cursed him. Major Nizar, a vicious officer, failed to get a word from him. Majid suffered a great deal of pain and torment until he passed away. He was shot by the officer."

Ali nodded and remained silent for a while with great sadness. "How long have you been in this jail?" Ali asked.

"I have been here for almost two years."

Ali shrugged, "Why? What's the reason?"

"Because I participated in a peaceful demonstration against the regime."

Mansour sighed deeply with sorrow and went on, "I haven't seen my wife and children since then. I'm most worried about my little daughter, Nadia, because she is autistic."

Ali nodded and kept quiet. He couldn't utter a word. He fell into an ocean of thinking against the music of prisoners snoring. *"Poor Majid suffered for his freedom, for his dignity. Unfortunately for him, his wife, children and his mother, didn't stop crying from the time he was arrested. I feel the most pity for his mother."*

With the first ray of light next morning the cell door was opened by the torturers. "Stand up animals!" one of the soldiers shouted. "Everybody out! Form a queue in the corridor."

"Ali Hussein al-Halabi," one of the soldiers shouted.

"Yes!" Ali replied.

"Come here, you bastard," another soldier said.

Ali went along with the soldiers.

He heard screaming while passing by the cells along the long corridors. He heard crying, groaning and moaning.

Suddenly, the soldiers stopped and opened one of the cells. It was a tiny cell, just three square metres. It held more than twenty prisoners, all of them women. Some of them were almost naked. Ali closed his eyes immediately. "Astaghafiru Allah", *"May Allah forgive me!"* he murmured.

"Open your eyes, idiot" one of the soldiers said firmly. "Our commander ordered us to show you this. We want you to see your women and what we're doing with them."

"Eventually, we will do this to all your mothers, sisters and daughters one day," another one said with a smile.

Ali could see three young women holding their babies. He cried inside, "Oh my God. Those three babies could be the result of the rape of those poor girls."

After that, Ali entered a torture chamber. He saw one of the prisoners was sitting on a chair made of metal, fixed to the floor in the middle of the filthy room. He could see nails, hair and stains of blood on the floor as well and on the walls. The prisoner was bleeding, his legs and hands were tied to the arms of the chair. There was a hole in the middle of the chair. As soon as the officer saw Ali entering, he placed a candle under the hole and lit it. The flame of the candle began burning the prisoner slowly. The man began screaming and screaming until he lost consciousness.

"Ya Allah! 'Oh my God!' What cruelty is this? This is a ruthless monster!" he thought with state of shock and horror. "Why did they show me these prison cells? It's really strange. It's really painful," Ali said to himself.

* * * * *

One of female prisoners at Jami'at al-Zahra, Mukhabarat Jawiya branch, managed to send out a letter with one of the sympathetic soldiers. The branch was full of prisoners from the rebel groups and their relatives. All of them were being subjected to unbearable torture and abuse. Most of women had been raped. The branch was well known for the cruelty of its officers.

Omar al-Halabi received the letter and ordered it to be read out in an urgently convened meeting.

"In the name of Allah, the most gracious, the most merciful,

I am writing these words with my heart wrenching. Please come to rescue us from this unbearable torment. We plea that you get us out of this Hell. Save us from the hands of these beasts by any means. Do whatever you can. We don't even mind if you demolish the prison on top of our heads. We would really prefer death to this life.

Most of us have conceived due to rape by these ruthless criminals. The virgin Mariam, peace be upon her, wished to die even though she knew she was pregnant, by Allah's word, by a miracle.

My heart has almost burst while writing this letter by blood because our tears have all dried up. There are babies as a result of the raping. Mine is kicking me and is due in a few days. If you're unable to free us at least send us birth control pills."

* * * * *

The Free Army groups, led by al-Nusra Front decided to attack the branch in Aleppo, whatever the risk. The centre wasn't too far from the rebel stronghold, being only one hundred and fifty metres away. Nevertheless, the branch was fortified and well-guarded with heavy weapons. It was obvious that a direct attack would be a very costly and dangerous adventure.

In the late winter of 2014, a group of around twenty al-Nusra Front members started digging a tunnel underground heading towards the Mukhabarat Jawiya centre under cover of darkness. According to the plan it would take about two months.

* * * * *

Chapter Three

Hunger as well as fire was being used to root out the Syrian revolution, which had sparked off in 2011. The revolution was against the Syrian tyrant, Bashar al-Assad, who had inherited the dictatorial regime from his father Hafiz al-Assad in 2000. Bashar's forces, supported by Hezbollah and other Shi'ite mercenaries, laid siege to rebel-seized towns and cities and prevented food, water, medicine and babies' milk getting through. Sieges were accompanied by the infamous campaign slogan 'Starve or Kneel'. Hundreds of thousands of Syrian people had suffered horribly in the sieges. Many areas and cities across the country and region, particularly their Lebanese neighbours, remained under deadly blockade for years with the regime blocking all ways and routes in and out of the affected areas, including, Eastern Ghouta, Wadi Baroda, Zabadani, Kafraya, Fuaa, Madaya and Deir Ezzor.

In Madaya, the siege was imposed for several months. The city completely ran out of food and clean water and people were eventually forced to resort to eating dogs, cats, donkeys and leaves from the trees. All routes leading to the city had been blocked by the forces loyal to Bashar al-Assad and by his allies and mercenaries, tightening the grip of the siege. A kilogram of rice was being sold for two hundred dollars by Hezbollah soldiers. Hundreds of people had already died of starvation and many more were now at that point. Bashar al-Assad and his allies also blocked any humanitarian relief reaching the starving people of Madaya. Horrific images of starving children, women and the elderly pulled at the heart strings of the world and drew global attention to the brutality of the regime.

The UN's hands were tied by the Syrian regime. The most the UN's humanitarian agency could do was to request humbly for the Syrian government to allow them access to Madaya and rescue the sick and starving people. Several times the request was turned down.

In this gloomy atmosphere, Fadi, a seven-year old boy, was dying on his mother lap. He was starving, having not eaten for more than a week. His mother, who had already lost two of her children previously because of starvation and lack of medication, burst into tears when Fadi became unconscious.

"Don't die, my love. Please be strong, my son!" she cried.

She then started running aimlessly, looking for anything in the starving town to feed her son. She looked to the sky and prayed, *"May Allah save my son. I have nobody else except him in this life."*

She then rushed back empty-handed with her heart aching. Her son was in a coma for few hours before he uttered his last breath.

"No! please don't die, my love!" She screamed and threw herself on his lifeless body. She cried and cried until she, too, expired.

* * * * *

Major Nizar was standing by the window looking outside, waiting for Ali al-Halabi, when the door knocked.

The officer turned his gaze to the door.

"Come in."

He looked at Ali al-Halabi and pointed to one of chairs. "Have a seat, Ali," said Nizar with kindness. "What would you like to drink, Ali? Coffee or tea?"

"Water please. I'm so thirsty," Ali said with a weak voice, surprised at the invitation.

"Hopefully nobody harmed you last night. I gave strict orders to the soldiers to treat you differently," Major Nizar said.

"Thank you, officer. That's very kind of you, sir," Ali said.

The major nodded and said kindly, "To be honest with you, Ali. I don't know why, but I feel some pity for you. This is the first time in my life. I even mentioned it to my commanding officer. Something very powerful inside tells me that you are different from other people."

Nizar paused for a moment, lit a cigarette and had a sip of the Turkish coffee that was on his desk. "Who knows? Perhaps it's because of your name. I really love my Lord, Ali ibn Abu Talib, and I love his name," the officer added.

"Thank you, sir," Ali said, again surprised.

"Anyway, I have a strong feeling that you are one of us and we can work together."

There was a knock at the door.

"Come in!" the officer shouted.

The waiter came in and put the tray on the desk before leaving the office.

"Thank you," the major said then looked at Ali, "Here we are: this water is for you," Major Nizar offered him the glass of water and pointed at the tray. "There's a cup of tea for you as well."

Ali picked up the water and drained it in one gulp.

"Shall I order another one for you?" Nizar asked.

"No thanks, sir."

Major Nizar nodded and said, "By the way, how is your wife? I am happy that she is pregnant eventually," he smiled. "It was a long time waiting, wasn't it?"

Ali was astonished, he feigned a shrug and kept silent.

"I know that you and your wife have had a problem for a long time trying to conceive children." The major added, "Your wife has got a nice name as well, Ali. Zineb is a lovely name. You know that we are also Alawites and love our Lord's family so much and we respect those who use their names."

Ali managed to control his anger, saying to himself, "It seems this dog knows everything, even the most confidential of details."

Nizar looked towards the window and kept silent for a few minutes.

"What does this criminal want from me? I know he's up to something. I know this is unusual treatment," Ali thought.

The officer stared back at Ali and continued, "Do you love Syria, Ali?"

Ali nodded, "Yes, of course I do, sir."

"Great!" Nizar smiled.

Then he paused for a moment and went on, "Well, then why don't we work together, Ali, to defend it. Let us stand by our nation. Our country is facing a 'global conspiracy' as our great leader, Bashar al-Assad, wisely pointed out at the beginning of the uprising. I will be straight with you, Ali. I would like you to be one of us. Terrorist groups have come from all over the world to shed our blood," Nizar confided.

He approached Ali and tapped him on the shoulder gently, continuing, "I promise you that you will be set free with lots of privileges and rewards." Then he looked at him straight in the eye, "What do you think, Ali?"

Ali remained silent. *"This is out of the blue,"* he thought.

The officer bit his lip to control his anger, remembering his boss's instructions, "I strongly advise you to seize this chance which, I believe, has come down from heaven."

The officer crushed the cigarette in the ashtray, adding, "I will tell you a secret: bear in your mind that this regime is not like others in the Arab world. Syria is a very strategically important country in the region and the superpowers will not let the regime fall. This is the reality. I repeat: this regime will not fall. al-Assad's family will rule this country forever. Therefore, please Ali, think twice and don't be taken in by those stupid terrorists."

"I'm sorry. I don't understand," Ali said.

Nizar sighed deeply. "Your future is with us, working for your country. If you agree to be one of us I will explain more and tell you what to do. I will tell you all the details about the job and the reward for doing it."

"I'm afraid I still don't understand," Ali said with confusion.

Nizar kept silent for a moment then said, "There's a task, which I believe will be very easy for you."

Ali al-Halabi lowered his head and remained silent without uttering a single word. He was in a state of shock.

Major Nizar frowned. He managed to control his anger, staring at him for a while, then nodded his head, "Okay, I will give you more time to think about the offer. It's not necessary to answer now."

* * * * *

Despite a large number of Syrians fleeing into Lebanon, the Lebanese government, under Hezbollah's influence, had not established any official camps or shelters to accommodate them. The Lebanese people, however, in Sunni areas in particular, such as Tripoli, welcomed the refugees and gave them as much support as they could.

In a two-person tent, in a gloomy and dull atmosphere, in the Bekaa Valley, in an unofficial refugee camp not far from the Syrian border, Salah, a six-year-old boy, opened his eyes after regaining consciousness. He looked around him in shock. To him it felt like a dream. He was unable to remember anything except the tremendously loud bang of the explosion in his home, then feeling an object hitting his head, whilst he was playing with children not far from his house. He looked to his hand, which was in bandages. He had a minor injury and some scratches to his face. He put his hand on his head at the place of the pain. Looking up, full of fear and in a shaken state, he could see only his uncle, Nouri, and his family.

The camp was not fit for human habitation but, nevertheless, was full of hundreds of Syrians. They were living in filthy, miserable conditions subjected to the cold weather of the winter and the heat of the summer as well as diseases.

"Where am I?" the boy asked, surprised, "Where's my mum and dad?"

Everyone looked to each other and kept silent.

He frowned and asked again firmly, "Where are they? Why don't you answer me?"

His uncle looked at him with pity and said with compassion, "I am afraid, son, they have died. I'm so sorry to tell you this, Salah, but this the truth."

Salah burst into tears. He began to cry incessantly. His aunt, Wedad, kissed him on his forehead, hugged him and said gently, with tears rolling down her cheeks, "They are martyrs! Don't cry, Salah, we are all your family. You will live with us. We will never leave you alone, love!"

He cried and cried…

"You're lucky that your neighbours rescued you. You're lucky, son. They were able to take you from under the wreckage. Your house was hit by a barrel-bomb dropped by one of Bashar al-Assad's aircrafts."

He kept crying. "I want my mum and dad."

Most of the refugees who had headed to Lebanon were women and children, who had lost their parents or guardians in the conflict. It was estimated that one and a half million Syrian refugees had fled to Lebanon. Despite the miserable life, Syrian children never lost hope of returning to their homes and their schools as they had been deprived from basic rights such as an education and to live in dignity. They played in the street, singing and smiling at passers-by but their eyes turned to the horizon in the hope that its haze would bring some relief. One could easily read the great sadness on their faces. And revenge started to fill their broken hearts.

Nouri's little one-year-old son, became sick. He had a high temperature and terrible bouts of coughing, which were getting worse by the hour.

"You have to get him to a clinic. He is going to die in front of us!" his wife screamed.

"We'll wait until early morning. Maybe he will be better. You know there are only a few mobile clinics in the camp."

"I don't want to know anything. I don't want my son to die in front of our eyes whilst we do nothing. You have to take him immediately."

Nouri finally went off to the clinic. He queued up for almost five hours, in bitterly cold weather in the open air, before his son was able to be seen by a doctor. He was given a course of antibiotics and paracetamol saying he had all the symptoms of pneumonia. Nouri returned to his tent at dawn, his heart aching. His wife showered him with many questions the moment he arrived, "What's wrong with Rami, Nouri? Is he okay? Has he been seen by the doctor? If so. What did he say?"

"*Alhamdulillah*, he is okay! Calm down, Wedad. The doctor gave him medicine and said that he would be okay in a few days."

"So why do you look miserable then? You look very sad and absent-minded!"

He sighed deeply and looked up, raising his hands and said with sadness, "May Allah destroy Bashar al-

Assad and his allies!" adding, "I saw in the clinic a three-year-old girl who was severely burned. She was brought from Syria because her house was hit by a missile. All her family are dead. It was horrible to see a child like that."

"Oh, my God! *Al-Wahash* seems to be serious about burning the country," she said, adding, "Is she still alive?"

"I don't know, she was unconscious. The doctor said that there was no chance she would live, but was still trying his best to save her."

Wedad nodded, wiped her tears and kept silent.

Chapter Four

Ali al-Halabi was profoundly upset, thinking about his ordeal in the darkness of the cell and fearing what was going on in the dungeons below him. He was totally confused. It had never crossed his mind that he would be asked to do such a thing. He sank into his thoughts, *"What a disaster! I never imagined being in this catastrophic situation. Working with criminals and helping them kill my brothers and friends. This is definitely treason and an unforgivable sin."* He sighed deeply whilst wiping away his tears. *"This is impossible! I will never be a traitor and betray my nation, whatever happens. I have to stick to my principles at any cost."*

He suddenly remembered his wife, *"I don't know why he mentioned my wife. Anyway, I know that I am not going to see her again and will not see the baby we've waited years for. That's my destiny. Tomorrow will be a very tough day. May Allah help me."*

The echo of the screaming of agony of the man who was burned by the candle was still in his ears. He also recalled the soldier's statement, *"We'll do this to all your mothers, sisters and daughters one day."*

He sighed deeply and closed his eyes with grief. Ali fell into a troubled sleep. An hour or so later he awoke with a fright and was anxious. He had dreamt that his wife had been arrested and brought to the centre. She had been subjected to rape and torture. She had had a miscarriage. He was looking at her, powerlessly, and was screaming at the top of his voice. Suddenly he woke up. He shook his head, trying to get rid of these horrific thoughts. "What a bad nightmare!" He murmered.

Next day, early in the morning, the cell door opened and one of the two guards said firmly, "Come on with us, you filthy dog!"

Ali al-Halabi was taken to the major again. Nizar welcomed him with a deceptive smile, "I hope you had a good sleep in a luxurious individual room."

"Thank you, sir."

"I think you have had enough time to think, Ali." Nizar said softly.

Ali remained silent. He lowered his head.

Nizar added, "Oh, sorry. I should have asked you: tea or coffee, Ali?"

"Neither, thank you."

"Do you know, Ali, that I told my boss that you are a good person and you will be willing to help us for the country's sake. I said this because I have a strong feeling, as I told you before, that you are one of us and that you're going to help us. So, don't let me down, Ali." the major said with mock-compassion.

Ali didn't answer and remained silent.

"Okay, although the saying is 'silence is a sign of agreement', I would like to hear your affirmative answer," Nizar stated.

"I ... I... I am so sorry, sir, to tell you that I cannot do that job. I cannot betray my – "

Major Nizar cut him off, "Have you thought deeply about the consequences? About your family for instance?"

Ali remained silent and kept his gaze down.

The officer frowned, "You bastard! Look at me! You have to know that my patience is running out."

Ali kept quiet and didn't reply. The major rose from his chair angrily all of a sudden and came very close to him. He looked into Ali's eyes. "Don't be stupid! You are pushing me to change the way I deal with you. Bear in your mind that you have no other chance than this, which has come down from heaven as I said before, and you must accept the offer. I strongly advise you to think twice!"

"I am sorry. I can't do it."

The major remained silent for a moment staring at Ali then hit him in the face very hard, bursting into swearing and shouting, "I know how to make you regret your stupidity!" He then bit his lip and hit him again. "This is the language you understand, you animal. I will tear your body into pieces and throw you to the dogs if you don't comply with my demand. You have no choice other than to submit."

The major then shifted his gaze towards the door and called two soldiers, who were standing silently outside. "Guards!"

They rushed in. "Yes sir!" they said firmly.

"Take this bastard and teach him how to respect his lords. Do you understand?" he shouted angrily.

"Yes, sir! Understood," they said in one voice.

In the torture chamber, Ali was subjected to severe punishment. He was stripped of his clothes completely, he was beaten with iron cables and heavy sticks. He was given electrical shocks until he lost consciousness.

An hour or so later, major Nizar entered the chamber. "What happened?" he asked the torturers.

41

"He is headstrong, sir," one of them said.

Nizar poured a bucket of cold water on Ali. He opened his eyes. The major put his foot on Ali's cheek and pushed his head against the floor and asked angrily, "What do you think now? I am still giving you a chance."

"No!" Ali answered with feeble voice.

Three other well-built men were called into the chamber, each holding a torture instrument. They stood silently staring viciously at Ali. The major pointed to them, shouting, "Those monsters are hungry for blood and eagerly await a word from me to tear your body into pieces."

Ali ignored him and remained silent.

"Yes or no? Tell me, you bastard. Do not be stubborn!" the major raised his voice.

"No. Kill me if you want. I will not change my mind," Ali said.

The major hit Ali's face brutally hard and he fell to the ground. The blood oozed from his mouth and nose.

"Teach him a lesson," the major said to the three men before he left the chamber angrily.

Ali, however, remained steadfast. The torture and intimidation failed to work and they were unable to change his mind. An hour or so later Major Nizar returned to the torture chamber and ordered them to fix his hands to the metal chair and place a candle under him and wait for further orders.

* * * * *

"That's unacceptable. I don't want to hear that from you, major," Adeeb yelled in frustration.

"I tried many ways, sir, but none of them worked, sir. He is very stubborn. He reminded me of his cousin, Majid, who died at my hands without being able to get a word from him. I believe Ali is the same," Major Nizar said.

"I understand from this that you have failed, haven't you?" Adeeb shouted. He stared at him and went on, "You have to admit that."

"Not yet, sir." Nizar said, pausing for a moment, before saying, "I only admit that I have lost the first round. There are many more rounds in the fight. I don't give up that easily, sir."

"The chief will not accept any excuse," Adeeb said. "Is that clear?" he added.

"Very clear, sir."

Major Nizar ordered the soldiers to untie Ali as soon as he returned to the chamber. "Take this bastard back to the cell!" he shouted.

Nizar returned to his office. He picked up the phone and said "Strong Turkish coffee."

He popped a cigarette in his mouth and was about to light it, when he heard a knock at the door.

"Come in."

One of the officers entered.

"Yes sir. How can I help you?"

"Call Abu al-Walid for me. I want the agent here as soon as possible."

"I will send him a text, sir."

"Bring all the information about Ali's wife and her family. I want the bastard's wife here before me."

"That will be suicidal, sir. She is in a fortified area in a terrorist stronghold and she is guarded by very tough fighters."

Nizar lit the cigarette. "I don't care. I have to bring her here at any price. Find me some brave officers for the job."

"I will, sir." the officer said.

Nizar decided to capture Ali's wife, thinking that she would play a significant role in putting Ali under enormous pressure to accept the offer.

* * * * *

From the time of Ali's arrest, Zineb al-Halabi, had moved to her father in-law's house, situated in one of the rebel strongholds in al-Atarib. Nizar would have no other choice but to go ahead with the plan despite the advice he had received that it would be a suicidal mission to penetrate the rebel's checkpoints. He was now forced to do everything in his power to satisfy his boss who would accept no excuse for failure. Nizar needed to demonstrate to his boss that Ali al-Halabi would not accept the offer under any circumstances.

Chapter Five

It was a dark, moonless night. Three members of the
Mukhabarat Jawiya, bearded and wearing clothes
similar to those used by rebels, were in a car on their
way towards al-Atarib. Abu al-Walid, an agent of
Mukhabarat Jawiya and at the same time a member of
Free Army, was their guide to Ali's parents' house.

"No one talks with the rebels, please. I will deal with
them," Abu al-Walid said as they were approaching the
main checkpoint.

"Assalamu Alaykum, guys. How are you doing?"
Abu al-Walid said with smile.

One of them looked at the driver and replied, "Wa
Alaykum Assalamu. *Ahlain,* Abu al-Walid. Good to see
you."

Another one looked into the car and asked, "Who
are those young men with you, Abu al-Walid?"

"Brothers! Mujahedeen. We were involved in a
mission," Abu al-Walid answered.

One of rebels lifted the barrier and let them in.

Zineb was lying in her bed. She was thinking about
her husband and her tears were flowing down her
cheeks, she was saying to herself, "I don't know if he is
dead or alive. It was his bad luck that he fell into the
tyrant's hands. He is now between the jaws of
crocodiles. Only Allah knows if he is still alive. I heard
him calling on Allah not to be captured by al-Assad's

45

soldiers. He said he would prefer to die a hundred times rather than be captured by those monsters."

She leant back on the pillow and went on, "I know for sure that I will never see him again. And he will not see his baby either. Only a few weeks away from his dream coming true. We waited years for this child."

She looked at her belly as she felt kicking from inside. She patted herself and whispered, "I know that you want to be out, darling." She wiped her tears and went on, "If you knew, darling, what's going on in this unjust world, you would prefer not to."

In the next room, Ali's mother was awake as well, crying and praying for her son's safety, "May Allah be with my beloved son. Protect him from any harm."

Abu al-Walid pointed at the house and said, 'That's the one, the one with the black door."

"Okay," the leader of the group said, "You have to wait for us here in the car, Abu al-Walid. We'll not be long."

Kamila, Ali's mother, whispered while shaking her husband by the shoulder, "Hussein! Hussein! Wake up. There's someone knocking at the door. Can't you hear it?" he gazed at his watch. "It's nearly two in the morning. Who is going to come at this late time?"

"I don't know. Go have a look," his wife said.

"Who is it?" Hussein shouted from behind the door.

"Assalam Alaykum, uncle Hussein. Can you open the door, please? We are Ali's friends. We have some news about him."

As soon as he opened the door, the three men rushed in. The leader of the group aimed his pistol at Hussein. He put his finger to his lips, "Shshsh. Not a word!" the officer hissed then he went on, asking, "Where is Ali's wife, Zineb? Where is she?"

"Who are you?" Hussein asked, frightened.

"Where is she? Tell us, otherwise I will empty the contents of my pistol into your head."

"She is sleeping in her room. Why do you want her? What do you want from her and who are you?"

The officer shifted his gaze to his two colleagues and ordered them to search the house. Meanwhile, Zineb heard the officer. She grabbed her mobile at once and dialled her father's number. Unfortunately for her, two soldiers broke into her room. One of them grabbed the mobile phone from her hand.

She started to scream but he shut her mouth by covering it with his hand.

Her father called back but there was no answer. The phone had been switched off. *"That's very strange for Zineb to call at this time,"* he thought. Omar then called the land line. Again, nobody answered the phone.

"Are you Zineb? Ali's wife?" the officer asked.

She nodded with great fear "Y... y... es, I am. What's wrong?"

"You have to come with us quietly."

"Who are you?" She asked.

"Mukhabarat Jawiya."

Ali's mother cried, "Please, leave her! She's pregnant."

"Shut your mouth, old woman, if you want to stay alive!" the officer shouted.

Ali's mother burst into tears.

The officer paused for a moment, thinking, "If I shoot those old bastards we will all be in trouble."

"Fear Allah! She is a pregnant and she's done nothing wrong. Please leave her alone! I will go with you instead," Hussein pleaded.

The officer frowned. He hit Hussein brutally with the back of the pistol butt on the head. Hussein fell down unconscious in a puddle of blood. The officer ordered his two colleagues to tie both of them up and put tape over their mouths. The soldiers also taped Zineb's mouth before leaving the house.

In the meantime, a rebel patrol stopped all of a sudden by the house when they spotted a suspicious car.

"Abu al-Walid! what are you doing here at this late time," one of the rebels asked with astonishment.

* * * * *

In February 2014, Dr Faraj Osman was abducted from his house in Damascus late at night by the regime's soldiers in mysterious circumstances. He was taken blindfolded and handcuffed, to an intelligence branch. He was beaten, kicked and tortured by ruthless executioners. After that, he was sent to Saydnaya military prison, one of the country's main prisons, used for holding political prisoners. The prison had been built on a massive site near a military base and included two large buildings, 'the Red Building' and 'the White Building'. In the prison, a prison officer interrogated Dr Osman.

"Look at this file!" the officer pointed at a large file on the table in front of him. "It contains all the information about you since you were born, including your activities with terrorists. You have to confess that you are a member of a terrorist group." The officer added.

Then the officer paused for a moment. He lit a cigarette, had a sip of coffee and went on, "I have no time to waste, bastard. You have to admit immediately that you're a traitor and a terrorist otherwise I will cut your body into pieces."

"I'm sorry officer. I did nothing wrong, and I don't know why I am here. I am a loyal to the regime. I've worked in most of the state hospitals for more than thirty years. I'm a well-respected doctor and I have been rewarded by the government. Ask my colleagues and my neighbours about me. There has definitely been some mistake here, sir," Dr Osman said.

The officer nodded, " You know Ahmed Jabber, don't you?"

"Yes, I do, sir! He is my neighbour. I have known him for long time, more than twenty years," he replied with astonishment.

"Why did you treat that dog? Didn't you know that he had been injured whilst participating in a demonstration against the regime. He's a traitor. Why did you help a conspirator?"

"I swear that I had no idea, sir," the doctor commented.

The officer frowned. "You bastard, do you think that you're able to fool me?"

"Please believe me, sir!" Dr Osman pleaded.

The officer smacked him on the face twice. He yelled with anger, "Liar!"

Then he gave him a statement and a pen and ordered him to sign.

"Sign!" the officer shouted. "Sign in front of your name, idiot!"

"How can I sign a statement about something I didn't do!" Dr Osman exclaimed.

The officer glowered towards the door and shouted. "Guards!"

Two bulky soldiers came in immediately and stood firmly in front of them. Waiting for the officer's orders.

"Take this pig to the welcoming room. Don't bring him back unless he wants to sign," the officer ordered.

"Understood, sir."

Whilst Dr Osman was on the way to the torture chamber he saw hundreds of dead bodies wrapped in sealed plastic rubbish bags. There were a large number of corpses piled in the corridors. He gazed at them half-faint, terrified, stomach turning. He closed his eyes for a moment. He became immersed in thought. *"Oh my God! what a sad view, what cruelty. Most of them looked like they died from starvation or disease."*

A few hours later he was taken back to the interrogation officer.

"What's your view now? Do you want to sign or not? One word: Yes or no?"

"Yes. As you like. I... I will, sir. I will do whatever you want. Please forgive me officer, I was wrong. I kiss your hand but please, don't torture me: I am an old man. I am diabetic as well. I need to take my medicine."

With a shaking hand, Dr Osman signed.

The officer sighed and ordered the soldiers, "Take this dog to the Red Building."

As he was approaching the cells Dr Osman heard screaming, crying and screeching coming from closed doors.

Suddenly, the soldiers stopped. One of them opened the door of the cell while the other one unhandcuffed Dr Osman and then pushed him hard inside, "Join these dogs!"

* * * * *

Abu al-Walid felt a cold through him. "I am waiting, Omar al-Halabi. We brought medicine to his daughter," he replied with a deceiving smile.

The rebels had received an emergency call.

"Okay!" the commander said. "Let's go back to the centre," he ordered.

Omar rushed to his brother's house when nobody answered his call. He knocked on the door and waited for few minutes but there was no reply. He was gravely concerned, thinking, *"Perhaps Zineb was taken to hospital for the birth."* he smiled. He was about to leave when he heard muttering from inside. He put his ear on the door. He was stunned. "There's somebody in there!" he said to himself. He knocked again and again before he decided to break into the house. He was horrified to see his brother unconsciousness in his blood. He took the tape off Kamila and asked, shocked, "Who did this? And where's my daughter? Where's Zineb?"

"The dogs of Mukhabarat Jawiya have abducted her." Kamila said with grief.

She threw herself on her husband and burst into tears. She was trying to stop the blood oozing from his head. Omar rushed to the nearest hospital, trying to rescue his brother. In the hospital, the doctor examined Hussein and looked at Omar and said with sorrow, "I am sorry, he is dead. He bled too much"

Omar glowered with grief, "Animals! They will pay a heavy price," he said with great anger.

Anas al-Shami, one of leaders of al-Nusra Front in Aleppo tapped on Omar's shoulder, "Be patient, brother!"

"Disaster! It's really a disaster. What kind of people are they? I can't believe that a human being could become more vicious than a monster," Omar said and went on, "The Mukhabarat Jawiya have also abducted my daughter."

"What! What are you saying?" al-Shami shouted with rage.

"She has been taken from my brother's house."

"How do you know it was the Mukhabarat Jawiya?"

"My brother's wife told me."

"This is a real catastrophe!" al-Shami said and paused for a moment. "How could this happen here in al-Atarib?" he exclaimed. "Definitely, there are some traitors amongst us in the city. We have to find them."

"Hundreds! Unfortunately, it's very easy to hire traitors."

"Anybody found dealing with the tyrant must be executed." Anas commented, nodding, "I'm with you, Omar, there are a lot of traitors amongst us."

"We have to find out who is behind my brother's death and my daughter's arrest."

"Do you know where your daughter is right now exactly, Omar?"

"I think she is in the Aleppo branch, Jami'at al-Zahra, where her husband is held. I am sure those criminals want to use her to put Ali under pressure."

Anas slapped his hands together in frustration. "We are scheduled to blow up the branch and there are only a few days left for that. We have been preparing the attack for about two months or so. I need to speak to the leader about delaying the attack," al-Shami said.

Omar managed to control his tears. "No! Don't change the plan, please. I would like to participate in this operation. I want to do the best to set free my daughter, and other prisoners."

Al-Shami wiped his beard and remained silent.

* * * * *

Zineb couldn't stop crying all the way to the branch. Fear filled her heart. *"Where are those monsters taking me and why? I did nothing wrong."*

"Put her in cell number nine for tonight," one of the officer ordered the soldiers. "Nobody touch her. This is Major Nizar's orders. He will see her tomorrow morning."

As soon as they took off the blindfold and tape she looked at the small filthy cell full of women. She was shaking uncontrollably and couldn't move: her legs were paralysed. She burst into tears. The female prisoners welcomed her, but with tears and sadness.

"Are you pregnant, sister?" Nawal, the eldest prisoner asked, noticing her belly.

Zineb was in a state of shock and kept crying. She cried and cried.

"Yes, she is. Can't you see her belly? This is a silly question, Nawal," Another prisoner answered. "I think she is in her last week."

Nawal hugged Zineb and cried, "I'm so sorry to see you her, sister. I feel pity for you. You are about my daughter's age. Please stop crying. You have to be patient. This is your destiny. Only Allah is able to help you. Grief and crying will not resolve the problem, my darling." She wiped her tears with her heart-wrenching, saying, "Sit here, love!"

Zineb remained silent. She was in state of shock and denial. It was a long and unpleasant night for Zineb. She didn't stop crying until dawn came.

Next morning, the interrogating officer was waiting in his office when Ali al-Halabi was brought in by two soldiers. Nizar stared at him, "Have you changed your mind, Ali?" Ali lowered his head and remained silent. Nizar bit his lip to control his anger.

"I am asking: have you changed your mind?"

Ali raised his head and looked at him, saying firmly, "No. And I will never change my mind. Kill me if you want."

The major nodded his head and said sarcastically "Really? Are you sure that is your final decision?" he added. "You are talking with great confidence," he approached him. "I have a nice surprise for you," Nizar whispered triumphantly.

Then he nodded and burst into laughter. He ordered the soldiers who were waiting at the door to come in.

Ali's eyes widened and his jaw dropped. "Oh, My God! What a disaster!" Ali said to himself, shocked. "This is unbelievable!"

Then he shut his eyes, his heart wrenching. He didn't want to believe his eyes. He shook his head. *"No. No. I don't believe that. She isn't here. This is not my wife. This woman is not Zineb. She's not! I heard a lot about the Mukhabarat tricks. This is one of them. I will not be taken in by this monster."*

Zineb also stared at him with astonishment then all of a sudden she burst into tears, "Ali!" she screamed. "He is not Ali! He has completely changed. Oh, my God! He has lost so much weight and his face is swollen from torture," she told herself.

Ali lost consciousness, unable to absorb the horrible surprise. The major poured cold water on his face. He opened his eyes and came back to reality and stared at his wife again. *"Criminals! Why have these monsters brought her here, why? She has done nothing wrong,"* he thought.

"A nice surprise, Ali, isn't it?" Nizar said, sarcastically, looking at Ali.

"Please leave her alone. She is a pregnant. She is an innocent woman. She has done nothing wrong. I swear."

Major Nizar approached her. He pulled her by her hair with one hand whilst holding a knife with the other.

She screamed, "Ali!"

He was lost for words. *"What a situation! What a humiliation!"* It was an overwhelming feeling of sadness Ali felt in his heart. Nevertheless, he was powerless and could do nothing. *"I wished I died before this. I —"*

"Now what do you think, hero? Are you going to agree to work with us or not, you bastard?" he placed the knife against Zineb's abdomen. "I will open her belly and take the foetus out. It's a good opportunity to see your baby, isn't it?"

Ali was distraught. He stared at the major without uttering a word.

Nizar eyes turn red with anger. "You have to answer at once. Yes or no? This is the last chance."

Chapter Six

Since the uprising had started, Syrian intelligence services had recruited hundreds of rebels in different cities and towns, using different ways and methods for confessions, including fear and desires. There was no doubt that the Syrian intelligence services had built up their experience of dealing with rebels and anybody else fighting the regime. They also had good working relationships with the intelligence agencies of other Arab countries including the Egyptian and Algerian agencies as well as those of Western countries, including the CIA.

Syrian intelligence services led by Asif Shawkat, played a significant role, in Hafiz al-Assad's era, in the interrogation of a large number of suspects who were sent to them by the CIA after the terrorist attack of 11th September, along with other Arabic intelligence services. Suspects were subjected to unbearable torture and torment in the Mukhabarat branches in Syria and information was extracted from them before they were sent back to the CIA.

Many agents had been recruited by the intelligence services, especially in prisons. In Syria, there are four security organisations that had been created by Hafiz al-Assad; the National Security Service; Air Force Intelligence; Military Security and Political Security. These organisations were given complete power and full authority to terrorise people in the country. Air Force

Intelligence became known for being the most violent organisation. As soon as someone agreed to work for one of those organisations as an informer or on other tasks they would be subjected to loyalty tests and exams. Those who passed the tests and exams were trained in the use of security equipment and devices and trained in the tactics and techniques used by detectives and undercover spies. They were also trained to collect information from groups and individuals on how to write reports afterwards, including analysis and filters. They were trained to avoid being spotted by others or bringing suspicion upon themselves. They were told how to deal with difficult circumstances which might arise during a mission.

Then, the agent was sent to live among the people. The intelligence services preferred to recruit wily, charismatic and personable, charming people or those who had influence in the community and they were willing to pay highly for specific tasks.

* * * * *

Ali looked at his wife in a state of shock and broke down in tears. "Please leave her alone, I will do whatever you want. Please don't harm her!" he cried.

"Good boy!" Nizar said. He let go of Zineb, put the knife on the table and went back to his chair.

"Now we can talk," headded with a triumphant smile. "Sorry! You forced me to do that, Ali."

The major paused for a moment and went on, "She will stay with us as a guest until you finish the mission. I promise you nobody will touch a hair on her head. Trust me."

Nizar ordered the soldiers to take Zineb to a VIP cell.

Ali nodded with confusion, saying, "Thank you, sir." and added, "What's the mission. I will do it right now if you want."

"Well done, Ali! But we are not in a hurry. You need to be trained for the task," the major said with a smile.

Nizar paused for a moment then went on, "I am sorry to inform you that your father passed away."

One week later, Ali prepared himself mentally to carry out the mission whilst the intelligence forces waited for an important piece of information about a meeting which was due to take place somewhere in Idleb or elsewhere. It was expected that most of the rebel leaders would participate in the meeting. Nizar thought, *"This is a golden opportunity to get rid of them all in one go. I will prove myself to my boss. He will be very happy with my achievements."*

The major tapped Ali on the shoulder and whispered, "Think of your family, Ali. It's time to prove yourself and rescue your wife and baby. I promise that as soon as the operation succeeds your wife will be set free. On top of that, we will reward you and help you to travel outside the country if you want to. I really feel pity for you Ali, but this is my job."

He paused for a moment and said, "Tomorrow night we will transfer you with three other prisoners to another branch. You will be given a chance to escape."

"That's a good idea. In that case, people will not have any doubts about me," Ali said.

"You are absolutely right, Ali," The major smiled. "I know that you are clever and will make it."

"How about the other prisoners; are they working for you as well?" Ali exclaimed.

"Of course not."

Ali paused for a while. "Can I see my wife please?" he pleaded.

The major nodded. "Yes, but not before you finish the job. Anyway, I assure you that she's fine. We have put her in a comfortable cell."

"Please I want to see her for a moment! I would like to comfort her! Also, that will inspire me to complete the task."

Nizar sighed deeply and dipped his head for a moment thinking, "Mmm. Okay, but only for a minute."

"That's very kind of you, major. I appreciate it. Thank you so much, sir." Ali commented.

"You can call me Nizar now. We have become colleagues." The major smiled and went on, "As I've said before, Ali, your mission is very easy and risk free. Your job is just to put in a small missile guidance device, a *chip*, whilst the leaders of the rebels get together for the meeting. It is not a difficult job, is it?" Nizar said with mock kindness.

Ali shook his head and said, "No, it is not a difficult job."

"We have received credible intelligence information that the terrorist leaders are about to have a meeting in the next few days. I assure you that nobody will notice the device. It's a very tiny chip," the major said.

Then he smiled and said, "As I said before, we will be very generous to you. And you have to know that there are lots of people willing to do this mission but I've chosen you for a reason. So, don't let me down."

"Thank you so much, major."

"Nizar! Please," the major said with a smile.
"Nizar," Ali said.

* * * * *

Zineb was leaning against the wall in the cell, her heart aching and her tears flowing down her cheeks. Although she was in a more comfortable cell, sharing it with just three other women, she was very frightened. She didn't know what was going on and what they wanted from her husband exactly. She wished to die rather than give birth in the prison. Having seen her husband in that state she immersed into an ocean of sadness. *"Poor Ali, obviously, he has been through very harsh torment and has been tortured physically and psychologically. I didn't recognise him at first. He had changed completely, he looked so pale and has lost so much weight. I could see from the conversation in the office that they wanted to use him against some people. It never crossed my mind that Ali would agree to be a traitor but he was under enormous pressure and wanted to rescue me and our baby in any way possible. But if the rebels find out they will kill him immediately and it will be a horrible disaster.Poor Ali, I know that you're under tremendous pressure. May Allah help you!"*

"Stop crying please!" one of the women said with compassion. "You're lucky to be in a five-star cell in this, the harshest prison in the country."

"Your family must have paid a big fortune to be in a cell like ours," another said.

Zineb looked at her and didn't comment.

"What's your name, darling?" the woman asked.

"Zineb."

"My name's Sarah. I have been here for five months."

Sarsh wiped away her tears and went on, "This is Sohad and Karema. Both of them have been here for three months."

"At least we are better off than the others," Sohad said.

Sarah looked around and whispered, "It's possible that if you are brought into this cell you will eventually be released," adding, "I stayed for one week in another cell with other women. It was a bad experience."

Sarah hesitated for a moment. "I cannot explain what I have seen. Horrible! Most of the woman have been raped. Some of them in front of each other," she lowered her voice, whispering, "They are animals. There is no mercy in their hearts at all."

Zineb shrugged and cried.

Sarah tapped her on her shoulder and asked sadly, "When are you due, Zineb?"

"The end of March *inshallah*," Zineb replied with grief.

"That's okay. Almost one month. I am sure you will give birth outside the prison, Zineb."

"That's impossible."

"Don't lose faith in Allah. He is able to do whatever He wants. He changes situations in a moment. Please, be hopeful, darling."

Zineb nodded and said, "May Allah hear you."

Suddenly the cell door opened and Ali came in. They hugged, kissed and cried.

"Abu al-Walid led the soldiers to me," she whispered.

He nodded and kept silent.

Whilst he was leaving the cell he looked towards the other women and pleaded, "Please look after her."

* * * * *

It was a lovely spring night. The sky was clear except for some haze here and there. The moon was full and sending its beams to the earth. Ali and the three other prisoners were being transferred from the Mukhabarat Jawiya branch prison of Aleppo to Palmyra prison. The driver switched off the car's headlights when he came close to the rebel stronghold in al-Atarib. Suddenly, the driver pretended to lose control of the car, which then hit one of the trees at the side of the road. The guards and the driver ran away as planned, leaving the car and prisoners. Ali and the other three prisoners walked to the nearest checkpoint. They told the story. After recognising them, the rebels helped to unlock their handcuffs and set them free.

Ali went to his house first. He placed the chip and the mobile phone in a safe place before leaving to go to his uncle's house.

Omar was sleeping when he heard knocking at the door. He looked at his mobile phone, saying, "It's three in the morning. Who could it be at this late time?"

He was surprise when saw Ali. They hugged each other.

"It's good to see you again, Ali!" Omar said in shock. "What a surprise!" He gazed at him, still in shock, "I cannot believe my eyes. Ali is here!"

Ali nodded sadly, "How are you uncle?"

"I'm fine. How about you, son?"

"No complaints," he replied with grief.

"What happened? How did you manage to get here? Did they release you?" Omar exclaimed.

"I was able to escape whilst we were being transferred to Palmyra prison." He sighed from the depths of his heart and went on, "The car collided with a tree. The driver was injured and the other two guards ran off. And we were not too far from the Mujahedeen checkpoint. They helped us to unlock the handcuffs."

Omar shrugged. "I am sorry to tell you that Zineb was abducted by the criminals of Mukhabarat Jawiya."

Ali wiped away his tears and nodded, "Yes, I know, uncle. Also, I know that my father died."

"I grieve over the loss of your father, Ali," his uncle said and went on, "How did you know that?" Omar added.

He managed to control his tears, "What a loss!"

He nodded, adding, "I saw Zineb. I saw her in the branch of Mukhabarat Jawiya."

"How is she?" Omar screamed.

Ali could not utter a single word. He remained silent.

"I swear that I will not sleep until I free her from the jaws of those crocodiles."

Ali thought to himself, *"He should know the truth. I definitely need his help. He is my uncle and her father and…"*

Omar cut him off, "What you are thinking about Ali? Tell me the truth, please. I can see there's something on your mind. I might be able to help you."

Ali nodded, "You're right uncle."

He sighed from the depth of his heart and told him the story and exactly what had happened to him with the interrogator officer, Major Hider Nizar.

"I won't tell anybody else about what happened. Please let people know that I succeeded in escaping the way I've told you."

He wiped his tears and went on, "You can't believe how many traitors are amongst us, working with Mukhabarat, uncle. Abu al-Walid is one of them. Do you believe that, uncle?"

"It's funny but I never trusted him. You know I have had doubts about him for a long time."

"Can you keep this between us, please? Because, if that major finds out that I've told you, he will take his revenge against Zineb! I don't trust the other three prisoners who have fled here with me," Ali added.

Omar nodded and said, "I guessed that they abducted Zineb to put pressure on you. That's why I didn't believe you at first."

"I noticed that, uncle."

Omar nodded, "Because I expected you when they kidnapped Zineb. But, to be honest, I never imagined that they would be so foolish to send you with this mission."

"They are not, uncle. It works sometimes, and they have to take a risk. This is a dirty war."

Omar frowned, "Tell me more about the traitor, Abu al-Walid. How did you find out that he was an agent for the intelligence service?"

"Zineb told me that he had helped the Mukhabarat to abduct her."

"No! Don't say that!" Omar said angrily. "He will pay the price!"

"That's the reality. I always wondered why he refused to shoot me when I was wounded even after I ordered him to kill me. He didn't try to rescue me either. That made me think that he told the tyrant soldiers where I was. Anyhow, he must be executed. I swear that I will kill him with my bare hands."

"Not now, Ali. I think if you kill him now it might cast doubt on you and your mission and that will put Zineb at risk. Leave him to me. I will do the job," Omar said.

"How can Zineb be rescued? That's the question."

"Please try to relax, Ali. Tomorrow morning, I will tell you how," Omar said, adding, "By the way have you got a mobile phone with you or any electronic devices?"

"No. Nothing."

"Can you tell me now, uncle? I don't have any patience. Please. How can I sleep when my wife is with monsters?" Ali asked.

"Unfortunately, I can tell you nothing. You have to be patient, Ali. But expect something will happen soon. I will let you know, in time. Be ready."

After some hesitation, Ali decided to tell his uncle about his son's ordeal in the prison. "Unfortunately, there's bad news you should know, uncle," Ali said with sadness.

"What's that?" Omar exclaimed.

"I grieve over the loss of your son, uncle. Majid passed away in the prison."

Omar wiped his tears and said, "I expected that. May Allah accept him as a martyr."

Next day, after noon, Ali called Major Nizar and told him that everything was going according to plan. The major was happy and informed his boss, Adeeb Salama, who immediately picked up the phone and rang Jamil Hassan.

"Hello sir, I would just like to tell you that we have succeeded in penetrating the enemy's security. Ali al-Halabi, our agent, is now amongst the terrorists and in contact with us. It appears that everything is going smoothly and according to plan, sir."

"Well done Adeeb, that's really good news. But do you trust him that much?" Jamil Hassan asked.

"No I don't, sir. But, his wife is with us and he knows that she will pay the heaviest price if he makes any mistakes."

"That's great. Now I can inform Mr President about the plan."

Jamil Hassan stopped for a moment, thinking. "Get rid of him and his wife as soon as the mission is finished. We don't keep traitors," he ordered.

* * * * *

Dr Osman stood by the door looking at the prisoners, downhearted and unable to focus. He was struck by a disgusting smell which made him forget his pain for a moment. He closed his eyes for a moment's relief. "Oh, my God! It's really horrible," he murmured. "They all look miserable, they look lifeless."

The inmates faces were pale and comatose. The cell was overcrowded with inhabitants. An ocean of eyes stared back at him, full of sadness and sickness. One of the prisoners approached him and said with astonishment, "It's very sad to see you here, Dr Osman."

Dr Osman nodded. "Who are you?" he asked with a feeble voice.

"I know you don't recognise me. I have changed a lot in prison."

He paused for a moment. "I am really sorry to have caused you such trouble, Dr Osman. Please forgive me: it was out of my hands, it was horrible torture beyond my ability. Please forgive me, brother."

"To be honest with you, I don't understand what you're saying. Who are you?"

"I am Ahmed Jabber, your neighbour. It was criminal of me to tell them that you had treated me. I wish I was dead before the day I had told them. Please forgive me!" he said with sorrow. A single tear slid down his cheek. "That's beyond my ability."

Dr Osman hugged him and burst out crying. "You really have changed completely. Don't worry brother, that's not your fault. That's our destiny, Ahmed."

Then he nodded. "I've been also through unbearable torture which was almost beyond human endurance," he whispered.

Suddenly, they were interrupted by the moaning and crying of one of the inmates.

Dr Osman looked at the man, asking, "What's wrong with him?"

"He's dying of starvation. We haven't eaten for several days. Two prisoners died last week."

"Why?"

"Every day people die from starvation. They don't give us sufficient food and drink."

Ahmed sighed from the depths of his heart and went on, "Death by starvation, under torture and lack of medicine is a normal thing here in the prison," he added.

"That's truly a crime against humanity. It's against the Prisoners Rights Law."

"They don't care. They don't deal with us as human beings." Ahmed wiped his tears and went on, "Be patient, doctor. We have no other choice here."

"Thank you, Ahmed. No complaints, brother. I was only thinking about my wife and children, I don't know what has happened after I was abducted."

"I hope they are okay. Most of these people in the cell have got families as well. They knew nothing from the time they were abducted by the regime. They have been completely cut off from any news of their families. By the way; what about my wife and children? Are they OK?"

"They're fine."

Ahmed then sighed, downhearted, adding, "Have you noticed that everybody looks nervous and frightened?"

"Yes, I did, why?"

"Because tomorrow is Monday. Every Monday, unfortunately, the authorities try some of the prisoners before martial court to execute them."

Dr Osman kept silent as he felt very frightened.

Early the next morning the cell door opened. Three soldiers entered and called out the names of three of the prisoners. The prisoners had been driven to their fate.

"Where will they take them?" Dr Osman asked.

"To the basement for trial. Or, you can say for death," Ahmed whispered.

"Why?"

Ahmed nodded and wiped his tears, "They have to get rid of people. As you can see, the prison is overcrowded and hundreds of new prisoners are brought here every day."

"Why don't they release them?" Dr Osman asked astonished.

"They enjoy killing. They love to shed our blood." Ahmed whispered with grief.

"Now I understand why there were lots of corpses and dead bodies near the torture chamber, in the yard and corridors."

"They collect them in certain places before they take them to be buried in mass graves on military land not far from here, in Qatana and Nahja," Ahmed said and added, "Tens of thousands have been killed by now and they still hang tens of prisoners every week either in this building or in the another one, the White Building. Also, there are others who die from the starvation, under torture and lack of health care. On the top of that, execution."

"How do you know that?" Dr Osman exclaimed.

He lowered his voice even more and went on, "I heard that by chance, when I was in the interrogation office. The officer talked over the phone when he was interrogating me."

"That's horrible."

Dr Osman remained silent. His thoughts summoned images of his wife and children. *"Forgive me my beloved! This is the end."*

A few weeks later, Dr Osman was taken to the basement with Ahmed. Both were sentenced to death in a very short trial, each lasting two minutes.

Chapter Seven

When the telephone rang, Jamil Hassan was in a meeting with his intelligent officers explaining the plan to assassinate the leaders of the terrorists. Adeeb Salama was on the line.

"Hello sir, I just wanted to inform you that we have significant information about the meeting of rebel leaders. It will take place in two days. Our agents will find out the place of the meeting. We will keep you informed about developments."

"That's very good news, but you must confirm the time and place precisely. We don't want any mistakes this time. Mr President is following closely the developments of this operation," Chief Jamil Hassan said.

"Understood, sir."

Jamil hung up and turned his gaze to the officers and said with a triumphant smile, "There's good news from our branch at Aleppo. Everything is going according the plan."

Meanwhile, Major Nizar was searching his mobile phone for any missed calls or messages. He talked to himself nervously, "Ali hasn't called. I haven't heard from him since yesterday. He promised to call me in a few hours but it's been more than twenty now."

Suddenly his mobile rang. He looked at the mobile screen. *"That's him. Ali!"*

"Hello, Ali. What's up? Where were you?" he questioned.

"Sorry Nizar, I worked hard to get the information you wanted. It was difficult because it was a closely guarded secret. Finally, I got it."

"Great. Well done!" Nizar shouted. He picked up a pen then said, "Okay, go ahead. Tell me."

"The meeting will take place after tomorrow, at two in the afternoon."

"Carry on! Where exactly? Tell me the location." Nizar said eagerly.

"Handarat's main health centre. Only al-Nusra's leader hasn't confirmed his attendance yet but there's some trustworthy information that he might join them ten minutes or so later, for security reasons."

"Great!" Nizar shouted, "Keep your eyes open, Ali. If there is any change or any further information you must let me know immediately."

"Of course, I will. How's my wife?" Ali asked

"She's fine. She's very well."

He wrote down the details and finished the call. Nizar looked at his mobile, smiling. *"Stupid guy! He thinks I am going to reward him for this."*

Major Nizar passed on to Chief Hassan the information he had received.

As soon as Jamil Hassan heard this, he gave orders for the Syrian Air Force to be put on high alert to carry out a significant mission at short notice.

* * * * *

After a few weeks of digging the tunnel, the rebels finished the task 3rd March 2015.

"Allahu Akbar," the leader of the group whispered. "Finally, we have arrived at the right point. The branch is now above our heads. We have to stop here."

It was a special night for members of the Free Army. Everybody was busy cleaning their machine guns, loading explosives and ammunition into cars, and preparing weapons. They were on high alert waiting for the leader's order.

Hani, one of the Free Army members, Omar's insurgents, was cleaning his rifle when Omar and Ali approached him.

"Are you ready Hani? Tomorrow will be a very tough day," Omar patted him on the shoulder.

"Do you know when the attack will take place?" Hani asked.

"I don't know exactly. But, any time from now. We are waiting the Emir's order."

Omar al-Halabi turned to Ali and said, "This is Hani Amen, from Idleb. He lost all his family in one of al-Assad's aircraft raids a few months ago, a barrel bomb fell on his family's house. It was completely destroyed."

Omar continued, "This is my brother in-law, Ali al-Halabi."

They shook hands and exchange smiles.

"Nice to meet you brother, Ali. I've heard a lot about your bravery."

"And I have heard of yours too, Hani. It's good to meet you," Ali replied.

"But I heard you were arrested by the regime's soldiers. Was that not true?"

One of the insurgents approached Omar and whispered in his ear, "We have captured Abu al-Walid sir, he is in a cell at the base."

"Excellent! I will be there soon, to see him."

Omar diverted his gaze towards Ali. "Let's go to the base. There's a surprise for you."

"What's that?" Ali asked.

"We captured the traitor." Omar bit his lip. "Let's go to see him." As soon as they arrived at the rebel's base Omar order the guard to open the door of the cell.

"Oh my God! Abu al-Walid. The traitor!" Ali screamed with astonishment. He approached him and punched him hard on the jaw. "Dog!" He cursed him and hit him again. He turned to Omar. "Let me kill this damn traitor."

Abu al-Walid began to shake, crying. "Please forgive me! Have mercy."

Omar nodded, "We still need him. We want to know about other hypocrites among us."

Next day, Abu al-Walid had been interrogated and executed as he admitted all the charges.

*****

Zineb was in labour when she heard a horrible explosion. It was such a powerful blast that it was heard in most of Aleppo City. The building's windows shattered on being blown up from underground and there were attacks from every side.

In early morning, the attack on Jami'at al-Zahra branch took place. Fierce fighting began after that in the centre between soldiers and the rebel groups led by al-Nusra Front. Most of the building had collapsed in the initial explosion and many soldiers and prisoners had been killed instantly, many more had been injured.

Sarah and the other women in the cell were screaming in a hysterical state, banging on the door for help. "Help! Help! there's a woman in labour here!"

"Not now Zineb, please! Don't push," Sarah looked at Zineb with compassion and shouted. "Please be patient, love, everything will be okay."

After tough fighting, Ali al-Halabi and some members of the rebel groups were able to break through the entrance after killing the guards. Unfortunately for Ali, one of the soldiers shot him in his right hand. He was badly injured.

"You have to retreat, Ali. You're wounded," one of rebels shouted.

Then he helped him to tourniquet his shoulder to stop the bleeding. Ali went on towards his wife's cell. He opened the door.

"Ali!" Zineb screamed with a feeble voice before losing consciousness.

"Don't waste time. Take her to hospital now. She's in labour. Hurry up. She and the baby are in danger," Sarah cried.

A few minutes later Omar entered the cell.

"Take her to hospital!" Ali shouted, as soon as he had seen his uncle.

Omar ordered two of his group to give Ali first-aid before he ran off. He took his daughter to the nearest rebel's mobile hospital.

An hour or so later Zineb gave birth to a boy at the hospital. Ali was overjoyed, he smiled and said, "Alhamdulillah, finally I have become a father."

Ali's right hand was badly injured. The doctor decided it was necessary to amputate it. Ali was distraught that he would no longer be able to fight the monster of Damascus now that he had lost his hand.

* * * * *

Chief Jamil Hassan was in his office. He was standing by the window, looking outside, very depressed and disappointed. There was a knock at the door.

"Enter." Jamil shouted.

General Adeeb Salama entered, saluted the Chief and stood still.

There was a moment of uncomfortable silence.

Jamil stared at him and shouted, "What a disgrace! Why has this mess happened? Can you tell me why?"

Adeeb kept silent, looking at the floor. Jamil inhaled from his cigarette, then turned to Adeeb and said, frowning, "Tell me what happened and how that bastard fooled you?"

"I'm sorry sir, the plan was going according to plan but the—"

Jamil hit the table with his fist and yelled. "Are you completely stupid? You have to admit that al-Halabi deceived you. Who is responsible? Who?"

Adeeb lowered his head and said, "Major Hider Nizar, sir."

"Where is he right now? Where's the dog?"

"Sadly, he was killed with our officers in th—"

"He was lucky, he escaped my wrath," then he paused for a moment, "Ali al-Halabi has misled us. He is behind this shameful loss. So, that pig must be made an example of."

Jamil Hassan ignored the telephone that was now ringing. An officer entered and said, "I'm very sorry to disturb you sir, but it's Mr Ali Mamlook, the National Intelligence Organisation Chief, on the phone. He wants to talk to you immediately."

He looked at Adeeb and shouted, "Dismissed!"

He picked up the handset.

"Can you hear me?" Mamlook said.

"Yes, sir."

"Can you explain what the hell is going on? Another failure?"

"Those terrorists used a new tactic, sir. They are ghosts. We could never have anticipated that they would attack from underground. We lost the best officers and soldiers in the Agency," Jamil Hassan replied.

Mamlook frowned. "Because all of you are stupid. The attack on the Aleppo branch is a shameful chapter in the history of our intelligence service. Our reputation is ruined. It's an atrocity. What do you say about this bloody attack?"

"I admit that there was a mistake, Chief. We never expected that at all, but I assure you, sir, they will not get away with it. I will make them regret it."

"Your apology is worse than the sin! You will have to pay the price" Mamlook yelled. "What a mess you've made, general. Instead of killing the terrorist leaders as planned, it is they who have destroyed one of our most fortified branches. They have really struck at our heart."

"I admit, that's very painful, sir."

"Mr President is very upset and wants to see you," Mamlook said angrily.

Jamil shuddered. "Ttt... to see me, sir?"

"He will interview you about your failure, prepare yourself for the investigation."

There was a painful silence for a moment.

"Come to my office and we will go to the meeting together. And make sure those bastards pay the heaviest price," Mamlook added firmly.

"I have already ordered our men to destroy al-Atarib."

* * * * *

An officer from the Republican Guards entered Bashar al-Assad's office, saying, "Mr President, Ali Mamlook and Jamil Hassan are outside, waiting your permission to enter, sir."

The President raised his head, "Let them in."

As soon as they came in Bashar al-Assad pointed to the chairs. "Be seated," he ordered.

There was an anxious silence for a few minutes. The President stared at them then sighed with frustration, "I'm running out of patience. Failure after failure?" he bit back his anger and exclaimed, gazing at them. He pointed at Mamlook. "Tell me, who is responsible for this atrocity?"

"There's an investigation underway, Mr President, I assure you that all those responsible will be brought before a military court, sir, and will receive a harsh sentence."

Jamil raised his hand. "Excuse me, sir, may I speak?"

Bashar al-Assad nodded, "Go on. What do you want to say?"

"I confess before you, Mr President, that some mistakes were made. Please forgive us and give us the chance to root out the traitors, sir. We assure you that such shortcomings will never happen again," Jamil said with grief.

The President shrugged and remained silent for a moment. He made no comment, contemplating his father's picture for a few minutes before shouting, bitterly, "Bear in mind that if there are any further mistakes you will all be executed."

"We still have the upper hand against those traitors. Just two hours ago, we attacked al-Atarib and other villages around Aleppo," Mamlook said.

"I will give you another chance but it will be your last. Any further failure and you will both be executed."

"Understood, sir." they both said.

Bashar al-Assad stared at them without uttering a word for a few minutes.

"Dismissed!" he shouted.

Chapter Eight

Russian air forces and Bashar al-Assad's warplanes and helicopters swarmed across the sky for several hours, targeting the rebel strongholds, destroying vehicles, mosques, hospitals and residential buildings whilst the tanks and rocket launchers rained down their shells, resulting in a large number of civilian casualties. Russian aircraft poured its lava of destruction on the area, to give cover to the regime and its allies advancing on the ground to recapture Handarat.

It was a fierce battle that was underway north east of Aleppo, close to the Turkish border, with the Syrian regime and its allies launching an attack on rebel strongholds. The Syrian Army, along with the Russian Air Force, Hezbollah and Iranian Revolutionary Guard Corps, backed by Shi'ite militias and mercenaries, used extensive force to recapture the area which they had lost to the rebels months previously. The village of Handarat in particular received a large proportion of the bombing and missiles due to its strategic location including Castello Road, a key supply route, linking Turkey and the city of Aleppo. The inhabitants of a Palestinian refugee camp, established decades earlier in Handarat by the government, was full of displaced Syrians, who had earlier fled the war zone, and who had been forced to stay in the camp.

By the end of October 2014, around four weeks after starting the attack, the regime and its allies were able to take most of the villages in the area including Handarat, al-Mudafah, Sift, al-Jbayleh and al-Muslimiyya. Only Castello Road remained in the rebel's hands despite being within firing range of the regime and its allies forces. One could see only smoke and flames cover the sky, joining the haze of the clouds.

A few weeks later, Russian forces intensified their attacks in Syria just a few days after Bashar al-Assad had cried out to be rescued. Iranian forces, Hezbollah militias and Shi'ite mercenaries from all over the world, had failed to stop the rebel's advance towards Damascus with their goal of getting rid of the tyrant, who had now been in power for almost fifteen years. He had inherited the country from his father, Hafiz al-Assad, who had come to power by way of a coup in 1970. He had ruled Syria with an iron fist for three decades before passing away. He had bequeathed Syria to his son, Bashar, who then followed in his father's murderous footsteps.

Bashar al-Assad formally requested the Russian government to intervene in Syria for the first time since the revolution had started almost five years previously. Vladimir Putin, the Russian President, had responded swiftly and immediately by sending his troops to Syria.

The bombardment and missiles unleashed by Russian aircraft on rebel stronghold areas did not stop for months and was particularly heavy in the north of Syria. Civilians were deliberately targeted. Ships of the Caspian Flotilla of the Russian Navy also fired missiles. Tens of Russian cruise missiles were fired into Syria indiscriminately, causing huge destruction and a large number of civilian casualties. Many houses were razed to the ground and many people were killed or wounded.

At the same time, the Syrian government's ground forces and its allies from the Iranian forces, Hezbollah and Shi'ite mercenaries from across the world succeeded in recapturing some territory in northern Hama and regaining other territory. Around two weeks after the Russian aggression, the Syrian Army and its allies started a ground offensive against rebels in Aleppo with Russian air cover.

* * * * *

Al-Atarib, a small town in Aleppo province, about twenty kilometres from the Syrian-Turkish border, woke up to the roaring of Russian aircraft and the sound of heavy bombardment. Russian aircraft released its missiles and poured its fire onto the rooftops of the houses.

"It's a raid! It's a raid!" everybody screamed.

As a result of the attack, more than sixty homes were destroyed completely, many civilians were killed and many others were wounded. One could only see fire and smoke covering the horizon as well as destruction. Blood spread everywhere. There was only the sound of screaming and crying as people were running in every direction, in confusion and horror.

Ali al-Halabi was very upset at being unable to participate in the fighting against the monsters any more, because of his disability. With great sadness, he decided to return to al-Atarib, his home town, to live with his wife and little son. He escaped several assassination attempts. One day he was in his family's house having dinner with his mother and two sisters when he heard a huge explosion about three miles away in the vicinity of his family's house. A few minutes later, he received a phone call from one of his neighbours.

"Hello? Yes, Essam. What's up?" Ali replied.

"Where are you, Ali?" Essam shouted.

"At my family's house. Why? What's wrong?"

"Your house has been destroyed by an aircraft missile. Was there anybody inside?"

"No. It is empty. Do you mean it is completely destroyed?" he exclaimed.

"Unfortunately, yes. There were lots of houses destroyed in the raid, many people were killed and many others were injured. Your next-door neighbour, Samir, lost his family," Essam added.

"That's really terrible. I'm coming right now."

Ali looked at the mobile screen and paused for a moment in a state of shock.

"What's wrong Ali? Who was that?" his wife asked.

He grimaced, "The tyrant's soldiers destroyed our village, Zineb. Our house is demolished. Samir Masood, our neighbour lost his family."

"Oh, my God! What a loss!" she shouted.

His mother clapped her hands together and wiped her eyes. "It looks like trouble doesn't want to leave you alone, my son. I told you that you have to leave this country. Bashar al-Assad's dogs will not leave us alone. They are desperate for revenge."

"Your mother's absolutely right. Please listen to her advi –," one of his sisters said and burst into tears, unable to finish her words.

He looked at his mother and said downheartedly, "I cannot leave you here alone, mum, you and my sisters."

His mother nodded and cried with sadness, "We are leaving as well. This place is not safe any more and I think what is coming will be even worse, my son."

Then she paused for a moment. "I can see thick black clouds on the horizon. I can see rivers of blood. I can see body parts and corpses everywhere. We underestimated the regime's strength and its relationship with the major countries."

Ali nodded and remained silent for a moment. He recalled silently, Nizar's comments about the regime. *"Syria is a very strategically important country in the region and the superpowers will not let the regime fall."* He murmured, "He was absolutely right!"

"What are you saying, Ali?" Zineb asked.

He gritted his teeth and shook his head, "Nothing."

He put on his jacket. "Right now, I have to go to the house. I must be there to see what's going on."

* * * * *

Meanwhile Samir Masood, Ali's neighbour, was digging in the rubble of his demolished house looking for his family. He stopped suddenly when he heard a feeble voice, then screamed out, "Who can help me? Who can give me a hand?" he was astonished, "She is alive! My daughter is still alive! Please! Please come quickly!"

Three men responded swiftly and they were able to get the little girl out alive from under the wreckage. She was holding a yellow cotton doll, an Eid gift from her mother.

Samir hugged her and burst into tears, "Alhamdulillah, you are okay, my love! You're fine,

Rawan, It's me, your dad. Don't be scared! You are safe, my darling. Please stop crying."

Rawan was only four years old. She was crying hysterically with great shock and fear, her eyes closed and face covered with sand and blood. "Mama!" she cried, "Where's mama? Where is she?" she asked.

Her father couldn't answer her. He kept silent as he was in a state of denial. Then he shook his head and return to reality and he said with enormous grief, "She will be all right darling, I will find her. I promise you, my love, that I will rescue her and your brothers."

A few hours later, Samir broke down in tears on finding one of his sons, two-year-old Mohsen, dead. He was cut into two halves. He cried whilst holding half of his son's body. "I have lost everything!" Samir shouted with great wretchedness.

He sat on the top of the accumulated rubble of his house and put his hand on his forehead, finally having lost hope of finding anyone else from his family alive. He became immersed in a sea of sadness and grief, murmuring, "May Allah shower his mercy on them. On my beloved wife and sons."

Essam al-Tayeb, one of Samir's neighbours, approached him, along with Ali al-Halabi.

"I grieve over the loss of your wife and sons, Samir!" Ali said with sadness and sorrow.

Essam nodded his head and said, "That is Allah's will. There can be no complaints. Be patient, Samir."

Samir turned towards them slowly, roared impatiently. "Why did this happen here? Why is that criminal Putin practicing his cruelty on us? Why is Bashar 'Az-zifat' killing us? Can you tell me why? Look at my house, razed to the ground. How can I get my wife and children out from under this mess? Can you tell me why?" his eyes were full of tears as he cried.

Ali patted him on the shoulder, saying, "Unfortunately, you're not alone in this chaos, Samir. Many houses have been destroyed and lots of families have been killed. Look around you... you'll see only a mess everywhere. The monster of Damascus and his allies want to destroy any area in Aleppo they are unable to get back from the rebels."

Samir paused for a while, searching for the right words to express himself, then shouted from the depths of his heart, "Monsters! All monsters!"

"You have to leave with your daughter," Essam said.

"Where do you want me to go? Can you tell me where?" he asked with grief.

"To any safe place, Samir. The criminals might strike again at any time," Essam answered.

Essam paused for a moment and went on, "I'm leaving as well. I have to find a safe place for my family. Syria is not safe any more."

Samir shook his head grimly and said, "I don't think that's good idea Essam. Syrians shouldn't leave their country to these monsters and vampires."

"I'm with you, you're absolutely right, Samir. But whoever can't fight and who has a family has no reason to stay here otherwise they will be a target for the monsters fire," Ali said.

Samir gazed at them motionlessly. "Anyway, there's nowhere to go. Russian missiles and airstrikes have turned Syria into Hell. There's nowhere to escape. And we don't have our passports: they're already lost under the wreckage. I don't have enough money to travel. On top of that, Rawan is sick. She is very sick."

He paused for a moment then he took a deep breath before bursting in anger, "I don't know why that tyrant would like to kill all of us, why he is destroying our homes and our country? We only asked for our freedom and justice. We are just humans desperate for liberty. We deserve to live in dignity. Where's the United Nations and the Security Council? Where are the Muslim and Arab countries?"

"They are blind and deaf. Don't wait for anything from the dead. They're hypocrites." Essam said.

"You know that Bashar al-Assad, doesn't allow anybody to express dissatisfaction with his regime. Do you remember, Samir, when I told you that Bashar al-Assad would burn the country if the uprising continued? His supporters made it obvious at the start, chanting, 'al-Assad aoo Nahraq Albalad', (Either al-Assad or we burn the country), 'al-Assad aoo La-ahaad' (al Assad or nobody is alive)." Ali replied.

Samir dropped his head and said, sadly, "Yes I remember. But the Damascus tyrant had not anticipated that the Syrian people would prefer death to staying under tyranny. Whatever happens, we are going to defend our dignity. Whatever the consequences."

A moment later, Essam screamed with terror, "Russian aircraft again. Look over there, to the east, Samir! There's an aircraft approaching. It isn't safe any more. Come on! Let's leave this place."

"Leave me alone. Please, just take your family and go," Samir cried.

"Come on, Samir, there's no time. Do it for your poor daughter, please," Essam, said, whilst continuing to look at the people of the city leaving their homeland and frantically running here and there. "I don't think anyone is going to stay here except the fighters who are willing to sacrifice their lives. I can arrange with smugglers to take you. I have a good connection with some of them. Ali al-Halabi and his family will be with you on the journey to Turkey."

Smoke and fire resulting from the airstrike close to the horizon filled the air, along with screaming and crying. Everywhere, people were running.

"Allah only knows how many souls this aircraft claimed," Essam exclaimed.

Then he paused for several seconds, "I will arrange with smugglers to help you to get into Turkey secretly."

"Thank you so much. But you know that I've lost all my money and I can't promise that I'll able to pay you back."

"Don't worry, brother. I'm not asking for my money back. Just go. Maybe we will meet in Turkey," Essam said with compassion.

Samir wiped his tears, "You're really a good man. I hope I can reward you."

Chapter Nine

The news of sunk boats and dinghies became a new norm, many sinking whilst trying to reach European Union countries. Some of the boats had been sunk in mysterious circumstances. Aljazeera, the Arabic news channel, broadcast a horrible image of a Greek Naval Officer trying to prevent people boarding a Greek Naval Ship from a dinghy full of refugees, mostly women and children, which had come close one dark, stormy night. Using a long, steel bar with a sharp object at the end like a knife he, the soldier, was seen to push at the dinghy whilst the passengers screamed hysterically, pleading for help. This tragic and inhumane action was a reminder of the shocking image of Alan Kurdi, a three-year-old boy, who was found lying face-down on a beach in Bodrum, Turkey. The lifeless body was one of more than twelve bodies of Syrian refugees attempting to reach Greece who had drowned in terrible circumstances. These horrible images and others stirred up a sense of horror and directed the attention of the people of Europe to the adversity and suffering of the Syrian people.

Nevertheless, thousands of Syrians met their destiny in similar conditions, their pleas for help going unseen and unheard. Most became food for the creatures of the sea, departing this life quietly. More fortunate souls were able to cross the sea but would face other types of agony and hardship. Shamefully, some Eastern Europe countries such as Macedonia, Hungary and Serbia treated the refugees with harshness and brutality. Several Western European Countries, dealt inhumanly with Syrian refugees. In October 2013, in one single incident, two hundred and sixty-eight Syrian refugees, including sixty children, lost their lives, about sixty miles away from the Italian island of Lampedusa. The Italian authorities refused to mount a naval rescue at first. The boat had sailed from Zuwarah, northwest Libya, and was full of refugees, with around four hundred and eighty passengers on board. The Italian authorities had been accused of negligence as they had ignored the SOS calls from a passenger from the boat, pleading for help, and deliberately allowed the refugees to drown.

* * * * *

It was a very dark, foggy winter's night. The wind was blowing strongly and the rain was very heavy. It was bitterly cold with the temperature below zero. Ali and Samir received a phone call from one of the smugglers. "Be ready tonight. The truck will be with you sometime soon to take you into Turkey. Don't bring with you any heavy luggage. Only small hand luggage allowed," the truck driver said.

Samir looked at Rawan, who was unwell, suffering from uncontrolled asthma. She was sleeping in his lap at the time. He wiped away his tears, with sadness before turning his gaze towards the horizon. *"May Allah help us in this journey and give my little girl a full recovery from chronic illness. YOU, Allah, know best that I will leave this soil only because of my poor daughter, otherwise I would stay here in my city to fight the monsters and vampires and defend my country. I never anticipated I could leave al-Sham, the blessed land."* He paused for a while as his gaze returned to his daughter. He stroked her hair gently then looked back to the sky. *"May Allah destroy Bashar al-Assad, his family, his soldiers and his allies and bring his downfall as soon as possible."*

An hour or so before midnight, the truck arrived. There was another family, a woman and two daughters, who would travel with Samir and Ali's families.

"Anyone who is sick or cannot walk for some distance cannot come with us. You should know that the journey will be very difficult." the driver said. "You have a tough time ahead of you."

Ali looked at the truck and asked with astonishment, "Are you sure this old vehicle will get us there?"

The driver glanced at him and said firmly, "Would you like to go or not? I have no time to waste."

"Of course I would," Ali replied. Then he went on, "But it is overloaded. Where we will all sit? There's no room."

The driver turned his attention to the occupants of the truck and shouted, "Squeeze yourself in. Make room for each other quickly." Then he stared back at them and went on, "Come on. Hurry up. We have to leave as soon as possible before we get hit by a missile or rocket-propelled grenade."

Then he looked at Samir, "Put your daughter on your lap."

Men, women and children were packed tightly into the vehicle, a Mitsubishi pick-up. As soon as everybody was in, the driver said, "Switch off your mobiles. Stay silent."

The truck's engine roared into life and set off. It was heading for the Syrian-Turkish border in darkness through the mountains and valleys. The driver seemed to be an expert who knew the area. He was driving slowly and cautiously without headlights to avoid al-Assad's air force and Russian aircraft which were firing on any moving object. Everybody in the vehicle was very scared.

Suddenly, the truck stopped and the driver hid the vehicle between some olive trees just as one of missiles landed and hit a car only a few metres in front. The flame lit the area. All the people in the car were killed.

Women and children in the truck began screaming.

"Shut up everybody!" the driver yelled, "We don't want to be spotted by the dogs of the regime."

Ten minutes later, the driver set off again towards the border. In the meantime, Rawan had an asthma attack and had bouts of strong coughing. Without her medication, she was coughing and sneezing badly. The driver stopped the car again and shouted angrily, "You have to shut her up. We don't want to die. I've told you that I don't take sick people with me. So, why did you come with us, you idiot? We are now crossing very close to one of the checkpoints of the regime's force. If they spot us we will be finished."

"I'm sorry. She's become sick all of a sudden and I can't do anything," Samir said.

The driver frowned, "You have to get out of my truck then." He looked around and hissed whilst aiming his pistol at Samir, "Get out of my truck immediately."

Samir pleaded, "Please let us go with you. Hopefully she will be better soon. I will try my best to keep her silent. Please don't leave us here in a ghostly area in this horrible weather. I will —"

The driver cut him off and didn't let him finish, "I'm not going to move an inch if you and your daughter don't get out."

Samir and his daughter got out of the truck. All the other passengers pleaded with the driver to let Samir and his daughter continue the journey with them.

Ali looked at the driver angrily. "If you don't let them carry on the journey you have to give him his money back right now," he insisted.

"Mind your own business! I'm not talking to you!" the driver said firmly, shouting, "Okay, get out of the truck as well. I will leave you all here."

Ali could not control his anger, saying, "If you don't take them, we will stay with them and we all want our money back."

The driver was silent for a moment then sighed deeply, staring at Samir, "Okay, but you must make sure that she keeps quiet for at least five minutes until we pass the checkpoint."

Samir nodded and covered his daughter's mouth with his hand, to stop the sound of any coughing. He cried inside, his heart aching. *What agony! I never imagined that I would find myself in this terrible situation. I have lost my family, my house and homeland. Now my daughter and I are going towards the unknown. We don't know what our destiny will be nor the difficulties that await us. We don't know when or if we will ever come back. Alhamdulillah, at least we are lucky that I have a brother in Istanbul we can go to after we get into Turkey. We can stay with him until we will arrange, according to the plan, to go to Germany via Greece. I don't want to stay in Turkey and be a liability to my brother and his family. Everybody said that Germany is the best European country for Syrian refugees and that Merkel, is the only European leader who has welcomed Syrian refugees."*

He then gazed upon his daughter and prayed, *"May Allah heal my daughter, help us in this long journey and give us the strength to arrive in Germany safely."*

Chapter Ten

At the end of October 2015, another round of peace talks were held in Vienna, with representatives from the US, Russia, Turkey, Saudi Arabia and Iran, which was participating for the first time formally on Syrian issues. Unsurprisingly, the participants, once again let down the Syrian people by disagreeing on the future of Bashar al-Assad. Two weeks later, a Russian plane was destroyed by a terrorist attack over Egypt. A bomb had been planted on the plane by the Egyptian branch of Da'esh, the so-called Islamic State, during the flight between Egypt and Russia. All two hundred and twenty-four passengers on board were killed over Sinai. At the same time, Da'esh also claimed responsibility for the Paris attacks which had killed two hundred and seventy people with many more injured. As a result, both Russian and French forces intensified their air strikes in Syria despite their differences on the issue. Vladimir Putin also issued orders for the cruiser, 'Moskva', in the eastern Mediterranean since the start of the Russian operations, to take part in the conflict. The French aircraft carrier, 'Charles De Gaulle', was also sent to the eastern Mediterranean.

The UN urged its members to adopt a resolution to coordinate their efforts to prevent and suppress terrorist acts committed by Da'esh or any other groups or entities associated with Al-Qaeda, and other terrorist groups, designated by the UN Security Council.

Inevitably, the relationship between Turkey and Russia broke down as the conflict over Syria increased, reaching its peak when a Turkish F16 fighter jet shot down a Russian aircraft bomber, Sukhoi SU24M, after two Russian Air Force planes violated Turkish airspace. After that, Syrian Turkmen rebels, supported by Turkey destroyed a Russian rescue helicopter, which was on a mission to rescue the pilots, killing a Russian naval infantryman.

For its part, the Syrian regime sighed with relief as its forces were able, with the help of its allies, to recapture Marj al-Sultan military airbase east of Damascus, held by one of the major rebel groups, Islam Army, *Jaysh al-Islam*, since the end of January 2016. Syrian forces also recaptured the strategically situated town of Salma, in the north-western province of Latakia. Other areas in the city of Deir Ezzor were also taken back, courtesy of the brutality of Russian Air Force fighter jets and missiles, which showered fire on the Syrian people. Russia provided Bashar al-Assad with unlimited military support. As a result, the regime was able to seize the mainly Sunni-populated town of Rabia, the last major town held by rebels in western Latakia province and then gain full control of the town of Al-Sheikh Maskin in Daraa province.

* * * * *

Ali al-Halabi and the migrants were asked by the driver, who stopped the truck, to get out and hide between olive trees until one of his associates came to lead them across the Turkish border because the truck could go no further.

"Wait for one of my associates who will take you on foot secretly into Turkey," the driver said.

"How long will we have to wait in this horrible weather, in the open air?" Ali asked with astonishment.

"Only a few hours until the way will be safe."

It was a bitterly cold night, with the wind blowing strongly. Heavy rain made conditions almost unbearable. Rawan's health was deteriorating. She had a chest infection and was trembling from the cold. Her father took off his wet coat and covered her with it.

"Only a few hours left. We're almost there, darling. I know you're sick and very tired. Please be patient, my love," he whispered and again wiped the tears, adding, "I will take you to a hospital as soon as we get to Turkey."

She stared at him and then said with a feeble and sad voice, "Take care of yourself dad, I love you so much. I feel that I am going to die any time."

"Please don't say that Rawan. I love you too. You're my life. Be strong," he said, his heart again breaking.

Two hours later, another smuggler arrived at the scene. Ali guessed he was about fifty years old. He introduced himself to the group, saying gently, "Assalamu alaykum, my name is Mostafa and I will take you into Turkey from here."

"How long will the journey take?" Samir asked.

"It depends on your ability to walk. Even though the distance is only a few hundred metres, we have to climb some mountains, which will be a bit hard."

"My poor daughter is so sick and is unable to walk at all. Is there any other way?"

"Unfortunately not. But we will help you carry her."

Then Mostafa looked towards the group and said, "Be ready. We will set off soon, inshallah."

Half an hour later, they moved towards the border, having received orders from Mostafa. They walked through a wooded area and climbed the hills and mountains.

Rawan was exhausted and her eyes were full of tears, showing utter sadness at the extreme violence she had witnessed, the airstrikes, the sound of bombing and the echo of her mum and her brothers' voices screaming under the rubble for help. That sound never left her ears. She diverted her gaze to her father when he asked her to stand up. Her eyes met his in silence.

"I can't, dad," she whispered.

He picked her up and put her on his shoulders.

* * * * *

The UN-mediated Geneva Syria peace talks started in the beginning of February 2016 whilst the Russian aggression continued and its offensive operations in Aleppo Province carried on. Sergei Lavrov, the Russian Foreign Minister, said clearly in Muscat, that Russia would not stop its air strikes until it had defeated terrorist organisations such as al-Nusra Front and Da'esh. A week later, after the Geneva peace talks had ended, militia fighters of the Kurdish People's Protection Units, YPG, captured a series of towns in the north-west of Aleppo, including Deir Jamal and al-Qamiya, as well as the former Menagh Airbase near the border with Turkey, previously taken by the rebels. In retaliation, the Turkish government shelled YPG positions near Azaz.

Meanwhile, the monster of Damascus and other vampires and beasts were enjoying killing and spreading the blood of Syrians all across the country, using lethal weapons. Surprisingly, NATO naval forces were deploying vessels and ships in the Mediterranean Sea not far from the Russian Navy that were firing missiles upon the heads of ordinary Syrian people. NATO members also decided to use its helicopters to prevent migrants crossing the water towards European coastlines. European Union countries were having meeting after meeting to discuss the migration of Syrians in particular and other people of other war zone areas including Afghanistan and Iraq. The goal appeared to be to block the way of anyone attempting to escape the savagery of war.

The UK participated in the operation, using a Royal Navy ship, 'RFA Mounts Bay', along with two other vessels, deployed to the Greek coast in an attempt to reduce the number of refugees flooding in from Turkey with the goal of getting into Europe. Turkey started to come under pressure from the European Union to stop the migrant smugglers operating in its territory. It began deploying more coastguards to intercept boats before they could reach the Greek coastline and to disrupt them even before leaving the departure point, on their way towards one of the European countries. At last, after many rounds of negotiations, the European Union succeeded in making a deal with Turkey to accommodate the refugees on its soil, following the refusal of twenty-eight European Union member countries to take more Syrian refugees into their protection. The European Union finally succeeded in its goal of making a deal with Turkey that would stop refugees and that would ensure Turkey received refugees sent back from European Union countries. The deal including a package of pledges and promises, including supporting Turkey financially.

* * * * *

The migrants continued their journey, each destined for his own, as yet, unknown destination, everyone carrying nothing but memories and torment, stories foaming out of their chests. Everyone wanted the entire world to hear his tale of agony and distress, how he or she had left their family behind, their homes and belongings. Not one of them had a plan about where to go, or when they would return. Everything was dull and dark in their eyes. They wanted only to leave the country for their safety.

Each one had to pay for the journey. Some had sold property or borrowed money from relatives.

Eventually, Ali and his group arrived at the Turkish border.

"Now we have to sneak inside quickly and quietly in small groups, before the first light of dawn. Keep your mobile phones on silent," Mostafa said.

He paused for a moment and added, "There is a minibus waiting for you after you cross the border that will take you to the nearest city. Bear in mind that although it's only a few meters separating us from Turkey we are now in the last and most dangerous part of the journey. It is the most difficult part."

Then he pointed his finger at a building, "See that building over there? That is a check point. It's only three minutes walk from here. But we have to get around it without drawing the attention of the security border guards in it. They are ruthless. Anyone who is captured by them will be in trouble."

"We have to get down this mountain and go behind the check point."

Samir shrugged in utter resignation, saying with grief, "I can't do it. My daughter is very ill, as you can see. It is too dangerous for her."

The smuggler looked at the girl with pity, "Okay, I will send you with the women in a bulldozer. However, you have to pay extra money for this service."

"I wish I had. I have no Lira on me," Samir said.

Mostafa nodded and kept silent.

"I will pay for him," Ali said.

Rawan and four women, including Ali's wife and his little son, sat in a container fixed to the front of the bulldozer. They sat on a sheet of clothes on the steel. It was a bitterly cold night, ten degrees below zero. Ali sat on a wing of the bulldozer's back wheels and Samir sat on another. It was a horrible downward journey along a muddy narrow path. The way was slippery and there was no light except a feeble light from the moon behind a haze which had spread across the sky. The rest of the group had walked down the mountain.

"Be careful everyone. Watch carefully where to put your feet. Anyone who falls or slips will be left behind. We will not stop to help anyone," Mostafa said.

"Come on, let's go," he added firmly.

Mostafa turned his attention to the driver of the bulldozer saying, "You have to go. Wait for us when you reach the bottom."

"Everybody must hold on tightly," the driver said before starting the bulldozer's engine and setting off.

The frame of the bulldozer was freezing. Only the driver was wearing gloves. Samir was holding the frame of the bulldozer, switching hands frequently to avoid becoming frozen to the steel. Unfortunately for Ali, he had only one hand to use. "It's really freezing," Samir looked at Ali with pity and said. "I am using one hand for holding and resting another to warm up a bit. How can you endure this cold, Ali?" Samir added.

Twenty minutes later, the driver stopped and said, "It looks like we are lost. I missed the junction. We have to go back. He looked at Samir and Ali and said, "Hold on tightly."

He reversed very fast. Everybody screamed. As the bulldozer was going through the olive trees, one of branches entered the container and scratched Rawan's face. "Dad!" she screamed and burst into tears.

Samir pleaded with the driver to stop so he could see his daughter and see what was wrong with her. But the driver remained silent and didn't answer him.

Samir thought with grief, "This is an endless journey."

Zineb hugged Rawan and comforted her. She wiped away her tears.

Chapter Eleven

Turkey, the only regional player against Bashar al-Assad, already had more than 2.5 million Syrian refugees on its territory and the number was increasing every day. Syrians were being treated with dignity and respect in Turkey. Erdogan, the President of Turkey, called them 'guests' and his government gave Syrian refugees the right to be educated in the country's schools, colleges and universities. Syrians were also given permission to work and live in the country without restrictions.

Historically, Turkey had treated Syria as a strategic locality. 'Al-Sham' (Syria, Lebanon, Jordan, Palestine) had been under the domination of the Ottoman Empire for more than four centuries. The Ottoman Empire had left Syria less than a century ago after being on the losing side in World War I to Alliance forces.

In May 1916, during that war, the British Foreign Minister, Frank Sykes, and his French counterpart, Francois Georges-Picot, had signed an agreement with the approval of Russia. The 'Sykes-Picot agreement', led to the division of the Ottoman Empire, particularly as it related to the Arab world. Shortly after the agreement, the so-called, 'Great Arab Revolt', ignited. The revolution, was led by Hussein ibn Ali, known as 'Sharif of Makkah', and supervised by Thomas Edward Lawrence, a British intelligence officer, known as 'Lawrence of Arabia', in the Eastern Arab world. Faisal,

Hussein's son, became the first Emir for what was known at the time as 'Greater Syria' and 'Syria and Lebanon', as soon as World War I had finished. Less than two years later, Faisal appointed himself as king of Greater Syria in 1920. A few months after King Faisal had ascended the throne, he received a worrying telegraph from French General Henri Gouraud whose ship had just arrived off the Lebanese coast. The King of Syria called an emergency meeting of his ministers, dignitaries and army leaders to discuss the issue before replying to the French general.

As soon as the meeting had convened, the King ordered that the general's message be read out. The demand was humiliating and included a demand that the King step down immediately and disband his army.

Ultimately, the King decided to comply with the general's order. Yosef al-Admah, the Minister of War, was against Gouraud's demand. He expressed his anger and proposed that the King must fight him all the way.

"It's treason! Where are their promises? We have to fight the French. We have to defend our territory and our dignity," al-Admah said firmly.

The King shrugged, commenting sadly, "We have no power to do so, Yosef. But thank you for your opinion."

Then he bit his lip and added, "Send the army home, Yosef, Dismiss them all."

"What do you mean, your Majesty?" the Minister asked.

"I order you to dismantle the Royal Army. Do you understand?"

Al-Admah nodded with sadness, "Understood, sir."

Once the meeting had finished, King Faisal sent a telegraph of compliance to the General. Gouraud, however, the General ignored the telegraph, with the excuse, later, that it had arrived too late.

Gouraud gave orders to his forces to move towards Syria to invade it. In the meantime, Yosef al-Admah along with hundreds of rebels decided to fight the occupiers at whatever cost, to the bitter end. A fierce battle took place in the spring of 1920, in Maysalun, about twelve kilometres west of Damascus, between al-Admah's soldiers and General Gouraud's forces. The enormous superiority of the weapons of the invaders gave the French Army the upper hand in the battle. Al-Admah, along with a large number of rebels, were killed in the conflict.

King Faisal left Damascus and hid in a village house, immersed in an ocean of thinking. His thoughts went back to two years previously. He remembered the days when he had entered Damascus, in 1918, in a majestic convoy following the success of the 'Great Arab Revolt', led by his father after the Ottoman Empire had been defeated by Allied Forces in World War I. He sighed deeply then bit his lip, saying to himself, *"Why has this happened to us? We deserve to be rewarded. Why did the French General invade Syria despite our submitting? We helped the Alliance to force the Turkish to leave the Levant of al-Sham and all Arab countries afterward. Our family played a significant role in defeating the Turkish forces."*

He leaned back in his chair and sank deeply into his thoughts. He recalled his journey to Europe with sorrow. He remembered how he sailed across the high sea waves by ship towards southern Europe and after almost a year he entered Damascus. The ship docked on the French coast coming from Britain after an official visit to the United Kingdom. He then nodded, saying to himself, *"Obviously, I now know why I received such a good reception during the signing of the final demarcation agreement between the Arab states with Chaim Weizmann, chairman of the World Zionist Organisation, in Paris, on behalf of my father, Sharif Hussein. It's clear now that it secured the conduct of all procedures to facilitate the immigration of Jews to 'the Promised Land' for preparation of establishment of Jewish state entity on the land of Palestine. Unfortunately, all that did not help us with these bastards. They were not able to defeat the Turks on Arab land in al-Sham and elsewhere without our help and support. Surprisingly, all of that has not been taken into account."*

Once King Faisal arrived in Hejaz, his father's kingdom, he communicated his resentment to the British authorities and complained about the humiliation he had received at the hands of France. Britain swiftly sent him one of its Royal Navy warships to take him to Iraq to be appointed by the British Government as King of Iraq.

The French General and his soldiers continued their advance until they entered Damascus without resistance. Gouraud headed towards the Umayyad Masjid, one of the oldest mosques in the world, built in the seventh century and located in the old city of Damascus. The General kicked Salah ad-Din ibn Ayyub's grave with hatred and said full of pride, "Awake, Salah ad-Din. we have returned. My presence here consecrates victory of the Cross over the Crescent."

Salah ad-Din ibn Ayyub, the founder of the Ayyubid empire, in the Arab world, including Syria and Egypt after the defeat of the Fatimid State in Egypt in 1163 had led the Islamic battles against the Crusaders and forced them out of Palestine and al-Sham State.

Four years or so after Gouraud had entered Damascus, Mustafa Kemal Ataturk, a Turkish army officer, fired the last bullet that finished off 'the Sick Man of Europe' ending the Ottoman Empire and the last Islamic Caliphate after six hundred years in power. As a result, the Empire fragmented into small countries. The Arab world also split into small lands and entities most of which became occupied.

Chapter Twelve

The bulldozer eventually reached the bottom of the mountain whilst Mostafa and his group were still walking down the mountain. It was very hard walking in the muddy, slippery ways between the olive trees. It was still extremely cold. Half an hour later they arrived and re-joined the group. They were cold and exhausted and dirty.

"Please, let us have a rest. We need a break for at least a few minutes to catch our breath," one of travellers said.

"We have no time. In only a few minutes you will be in Turkey, where you can have a rest for as long as you want," Mostafa said.

Mostafa then divided the group into smaller groups, four in each. He looked at Samir and said, "Now the first group must sneak across via these olive trees. You and your daughter will have to walk only few metres and you will be in Turkey."

Then he spoke to two men, pointing, "You and you, both of you accompany Samir and his daughter just in case she needs help." He then added, "Keep going until you see a green and white minibus with the Turkish flag parked between the trees. You can't miss it. Someone will meet you there."

There was an echo of the sound of shooting coming from a distance all of a sudden, penetrating the silence of the night. Everybody was scared and anxious.

"Be calm! don't worry, they are shooting at other groups trying to cross the border from the other side. You're on the safe side. Just keep going." Mostafa said, smiling, whilst boarding the bulldozer to return.

Then he waved and wished them good luck. "Goodbye."

Everybody waved back.

All the group succeeded in crossing the border safely. Samir sighed deeply with relief as he boarded the minibus. He kissed his daughter, whispering, "Alhamdulillah, finally we are in Turkey, darling. We will go to your uncle's house. He will take care of us, love. You will forget this torment and play with his children. Just a bit more patience. You're a very brave girl."

Rawan kept looking at him with very tired eyes. She smiled and remained silent.

The minibus set off, when everybody had got in, heading towards the nearest Turkish city, Ghazi-Intab, the last stop of the journey. Rawan had been seen by a doctor in the refugee camp. The doctor gave her an inhaler and coughing syrup. Three days later, Samir and his daughter made their way towards Istanbul.

Emad, Samir's brother and his family welcomed them. Rawan, soon suffered a severe asthma attack and fell ill again, the medicine not appearing to work. She was admitted to a hospital in Istanbul and diagnosed with severe pneumonia. Her health deteriorated day by day. She began to lose a lot of weight and had no appetite. She was coughing badly and had bouts of asthma attacks. The doctors prescribed the strongest dose of antibiotics and a nurse gave her injections. Samir put his hand on his daughter's forehead. "What's wrong with her, doctor?" he asked nervously. "Her temperature is so high as well. Why doesn't she respond to the treatment?"

The doctor shrugged and said, "She is in a really critical condition."

"Please, doctor, do whatever you can to rescue her. She is the only member of my family left," Samir pleaded; wiping a tear that was rolling down his cheek.

The doctor nodded and said, "Of course. I will do my best."

Samir kissed Rawan on her cheek and said with eyes yet again full of tears, "You will be okay soon, love."

"Take care of yourself, dad, I love you! I'm going to my mum and brothers. I am departing," She said with a feeble voice.

"Don't say that, darling, I need you here with me."

* * * * *

On the fifth anniversary of the rebellion, Putin suddenly announced that his forces would be withdrawing from Syria. He declared that the Russian mission had been completed. In reality, his air force continued bombing everywhere in Syria. Seemingly, the Russian president became addicted to Syrian blood. Up to that date, at least five hundred thousand Syrian people had been killed and a huge number had been wounded, with more than half of the Syrian population of the country being displaced or forced to emigrate. The huge scale of the Russian intervention had only succeeded in fuelling the rebellion and pouring oil on fire.

In the spring of 2016, Da'esh was defeated by the regime soldiers backed by Russian air forces and

Hezbollah militias and forced out of Palmyra, the archaeological city. Bashar al-Assad's triumph in the city was welcomed by the European Union and other countries. A few weeks later, al-Nusra Front supported by the Syrian Free Army groups recaptured strategic villages, in the south of Aleppo and other areas from the regime they had lost a few months previously during the Russian aggression and heavy airstrikes. Al-Nusra Front also seized more than a dozen Hezbollah fighters and kept them hostage in the battle before withdrawing under pressure from a Russian airstrike which used phosphoric bombs. The rebels had initiated a new strategy in the conflict of 'hit and run' replacing the strategy of holding territory, which had become too difficult and costly under the lava of Russian aircraft and missiles.

* * * * *

It was quiet and gloomy and the sky was dull. There was only the smell of the salt of the sea and the sound of the waves. Two smugglers on the coast of Izmir in western Turkey stood on the shore on a dark chilly night, working very hard against time, inflating a rubber boat and fixing an engine to it. As soon as they finished preparing the dinghy they sent a text message to their colleagues. "Come on. It's ready to go."

Ali al-Halabi, as well as other migrants, received the message on their mobiles. Ali had prepared his family for this unsafe adventure.

His wife asked. "Are you sure it will be a safe journey, Ali?"

He nodded and said sadly, "There's no guarantee, Zineb. But we are lucky that the sea is fine tonight, despite the wind. Anyway, we have to go. We should take a risk. We are running out of money and there's no work for me here."

Essam al-Tayeb also told his wife about the smugglers message he had received. "We have to be ready with the children. I have just received, at short notice, the signal to move towards the beach, the starting point of the journey towards Europe in half an hour maximum."

"Half an hour? That's such a short period. Can you get the children dressed, please?" she said, urgently.

She looked at him with surprise, asking, "To be honest with you Essam, I don't know what you are doing."

He kept silent.

"Why are you inflating a balloon? It's really strange. We don't have time to play with balloons. You drive me mad!" she yelled.

Ignoring her, he opened the spout of the balloon widely and pushed his mobile phone inside. After that he let the air out before tightening it. Then he turned to his wife and said, "This is the most important thing in the journey, Wafa," he smiled. "Now my phone is safe. The balloon will keep it waterproof. Just in case anything goes wrong in the water, at least we can call for rescue."

They heard crying.

"Fathi needs to be fed," Wafa said.

"Okay, Wafa, I will get the children dressed. Go and feed him. Hurry up!"

About sixty people, most of them women and children, rushed to the dinghy. They began boarding it.

"Squeeze yourselves in quickly!" one of the smugglers shouted, "All of you must board it as quickly as possible."

Ali looked at the dinghy and said to himself, "Is this the boat that will take all of us? That's impossible. Are they mad?"

Then he turned his gaze to one of smugglers and protested, "This is too small for all these people."

The smuggler shrugged and ignored Ali's comments. He went on with his advice to the boarders, "You have to put the children and women in the middle of the boat. Men should sit on the edges. Take care of your belongings. Your mobile phones must be switched off during the journey."

"We are human beings. We are not animals. We paid a lot of money for this journey. It's not fair. You shouldn't think only about money," Ali angrily said.

"If you're not happy to go with us you can stay here. We don't force people to travel."

Ali frowned. He looked at his wife and asked her, "What do you think, Zineb? We still have a chance to stay in Turkey. To be honest with you, I am not happy with this journey."

His wife nodded, "Let's go, Ali. We have no other choice. We don't want to regret it one day. It's for our son's future. We have to sacrifice. We've waited two months for this moment. I think we have to take the risk. It's only a few hours sailing and we'll be in Europe."

The smuggler pointed towards Greece and said, "Look over there at that light. We are going to go there.

That is a small Greek island called Farmakonisi. It is not very far from here. It is only a few kilometres away. You have to be patient for only a few hours."

Everybody boarded the dinghy except Ali and his family.

The driver looked at them and said, "Are you coming with us or not? We are leaving right now."

Ali al-Halabi shrugged and said, "Yes, we are."

He prayed whilst boarding the dinghy, "May Allah, make it an easy journey for us."

"Make sure that all mobile phones are switched off. Everybody must wear a safety jacket. Hold babies tightly. We are going to set off," the dinghy's pilot announced as everybody boarded.

The dinghy was launched into the water without starting the engine at once. The smugglers rowed for two hundred metres or so away from the coast. Finally, the dinghy's engine roared into life and they set off as quickly as possible towards their dream land.

It was a long journey for Essam and his family as well as the other refugees on board. Most of them were seasick. They were happy when they came close to the island. They were only few hundred metres away when the boat's engine stopped suddenly and they realised it had broken down. The driver could not restart the engine despite many attempts. A few minutes later a small rubber boat approached them. The driver jumped into it and returned to the Turkish coast. The migrants were left to their destiny. Unfortunately for them, the waves began to rise higher and the boat eventually lost its balance and became like a leaf in the wind. One could only hear the crying and screaming of the women and children.

Essam tried to make an emergency call on his mobile. He rang his cousin in London for help. He looked at his mobile and said to himself, "Oh my God! There's no answer."

"What's wrong?" Wafa screamed.

"No answer. Hitham isn't picking up the phone. It's so late there at the moment. It's after midnight in the UK now. I don't think he will answer."

"Try again, Essam. Don't give up. We don't want to die in the water." She cried.

In his bed in London, Hitham looked at the clock on the mobile screen and switched it off and went back to sleep.

"Who's that ringing at this time, Hitham?" his wife asked, surprised.

"I don't know. There's no caller identity."

"You should answer. Maybe someone needs you urgently."

In the boat, Essam, said with despair, tears springing in his eyes, "He switched his mobile off. We have lost our last hope."

"Try again!" Wafa cried. "We have to rescue our children."

He kept trying. As soon as Hitham switched on his mobile again it rang.

"Hello Hitham. I'm Essam, your cousin. Can you hear me."

"Yes! Go ahead. I'm all ears."

"We are sinking, we are going to die. Please, Hitham, do something. Help us please!" Essam shouted.

Hitham was shocked. He leaned on the wall, confused.

"Okay! I will," Hitham said. "Where are you exactly? What's going on? Calm down and tell me."

"We are in the water. Only several hundred metres away from Farmakonisi, one of the Greek islands. We can see it clearly. It's not too far from here. But our boat has broken down. Call the Turkish authorities, to save our lives!" Essam cried.

"Essam, please be strong. Be determined. Hold your children tightly," Hitham said. "And keep in touch. I will call you back."

"Please, quickly, we're running out of time. Any delay and we will be finished."

Hitham contacted some of the human rights organisation in Turkey immediately and told them what was happening to the migrants boat. He gave them the boat's location and all the details they needed. Also, the Turkish authority were informed.

Suddenly, a Turkish vessel appeared. It was coming towards them to rescue them. Everybody in the boat started waving to the Turkish boat as it was approaching. Unfortunately for them, the boat stopped all of a sudden.

Essam looked at Ali and protested with frustration, "What's happened? Why has the Turkish boat stopped?" then went on, "They are watching us die."

Everybody was working very hard to empty the boat of incoming water. But they were failing and the boat was becoming heavier. Four men jumped into the water to try to prevent it sinking. The Turkish boat was unable to go any further as the migrants boat had already entered Greek territorial waters. Nevertheless, the Greek government had been informed about the boat.

* * * * *

Rawan closed her eyes to have some rest and fell into a deep sleep. Her father, who was beside her bed, covered her to her chin with a white sheet before he left to the waiting room. He was crying silently and supplicated Allah to heal his daughter.

In a dream, Rawan received an invitation to her mother's palace in heaven. Rawan was wearing a wedding-dress and a gold crown embellished with diamonds. On entering the palace, she saw her mother sitting in a gorgeous garden, full of flowers, roses and lush grass. Rawan could see wonderful colourful birds flying around and singing a lovely song the like of which she had never heard in her entire life. Her mother was wearing a rose-coloured, long silk dress and both of her brothers were sitting beside their mother. One could see the happiness and joy lighting their faces. They were dressed in lovely, bright green clothes. Their aroma was covering the garden. Her mother stood up quickly on seeing her daughter. She opened her arms and ran towards Rawan.

"Rawan, come on here, love, I'm your mother!"

Rawan ran towards her mother. They hugged each other and kissed.

"I missed you, love," her mother said with joy.

"I missed you too, mum," Rawan said.

Rawan nodded whilst looking at her from head to toe in astonishment, "Wow! You look so beautiful mum and even younger!"

"Thank you darling!" her mum smiled, gazing around. "Where's your dad, where's Samir? Rawan? I can't see him with you."

"He is in —"

Suddenly, Rawan opened her eyes on hearing the nurse's voice, "Rawan! Rawan! Wake up! It is medicine time, darling."

Rawan opened her eyes slowly. She was looking at her father and said with a feeble voice, "I had a really nice dream, dad, I wish I hadn't woken up."

She paused for a moment before continuing, her tongue very heavy, "Mm... my mum is waiting. Goodbye da —"

She couldn't finish her words and she breathed her last.

"Rawaaaan!" Samir shouted.

The doctor came into the room. He examined her then turned slowly towards Samir, saying, "I am so sorry, sir. Your daughter has passed away."

Samir broke down in tears. He kissed her on the forehead, saying sadly, "Goodbye love! You have suffered a lot, Rawan."

Emad went to the hospital as soon as he heard that Rawan had passed away.

"Be patient, brother," Emad said, placing his hand on his brother's shoulder saying with grief. "This is Allah's will, we have to accept it, brother."

Samir looked at his brother. "I have lost everything. My entire life has become bitter and tasteless. Rawan has gone, Emad," he said with great sadness. "Do you know what this means for me?" he cried, tears streaming down his face.

Emad nodded and remained silent.

Samir frowned, he brushed his tears away. "I have to return to take revenge against the criminals. I have to fight the monsters all the way. I have nothing else to lose," he shouted before breaking down in tears again.

Chapter Thirteen

There was very heavy security in al-Mazah in Damascus, around the President's residential 'Republican Palace'. One could see the heavy presence of tanks, anti-aircraft battery missiles and a large number of Republic Guard Forces surrounding the palace. There were checkpoints and barriers on every road that lead to it. Iranian Revolutionary Guard and Hezbollah militia were deployed in the capital as well. Al-Assad's family were inside the palace receiving condolences from delegations and officials. Anissa Makhlouf, the President's mother had passed away, having been ill for many years.

The President was sitting beside his brother, Maher, in a deeply sad state, "I don't know what's going on, Maher. I never thought we would actually lose our mother. I think this year will be very tough for us," Bashar al-Assad whispered.

"What a loss! She was a great woman."

Maher's shoulders slumped and he continued, whilst trying to control his emotions, "She suffered a lot of pain and agony for many years."

"We wish her to sleep in peace and have a good passing! May God incarnate her soul in a good creature," Bashar al-Assad commented and went on, "Everything has become gloomy and dark in my eyes. Nothing goes according to my wishes. To be honest, I don't trust anybody," he said.

There was a moment of silence and grief.

"What's up, Bashar? Why are you so pessimistic?" Maher asked.

Bashar al-Assad frowned, "We have to admit that we are losing. We lost control of the country. There are some intelligence reports that Russia is thinking about making a deal with the US and withdrawing its troops or part of its forces, at least. Honestly, my brother, I don't know what's going on."

"I think the US and Russians are up to something. I told you from the beginning that Russia only cares about its own interests. Iran has a great interest in Syria as well, but in my opinion the Persian state, I mean Iran, is closer to us than Russia and we have a lot in common with the Iranians despite the fact that I don't like Iranian leaders. In fact, Iran suffered a great deal in Syria and lost many of its elite soldiers and officers of the Revolutionary Guard and they've lost a lot of money in the region," Maher al-Assad said.

"I know everybody has his own interests in Syria. But it's very hard to satisfy everyone. Iran had a dream of a Shi'ite empire, a Safawi state, in al-Sham. Anyway, we are caught in the global crossfire of interests. We don't know who is with us and who is against us."

He paused for a moment and added, "We all know who holds the keys."

"Do you mean Israel?" Maher al-Assad exclaimed.

The president nodded, "Yes, I do."

There was another uncomfortable moment of silence.

"What's the plan then, Bashar? I am really confused," Maher asked.

The President was resigned, "Of course, we have to fight until the last drop of our blood. I promised my parents that I would never give up our country."

Bashar remained silent for a moment. "By the way, Maher, please can you hide your dissatisfaction. Don't show your hatred to the leaders of the Iranian Revolutionary Guard and Hezbollah. You know we are at their mercy at the moment."

Maher frowned, "Why are they treating us like slaves? This is our country."

Bashar al-Assad stared at him and kept silent.

Maher nodded with grief and went on, "You were completely wrong to call for them to help us in the first place. We had protection from the Western countries, who promised to keep us in power forever. Thanks to our great father who had prepared that for us."

"We needed them to fight with us at this stage as our army was exhausted. We had already lost most of our troops in the bloody war," replied the President.

"Frankly, I can't stand them at all. I hate them with every fibre of my being," Maher said.

"I know but our interests converge. And as for us, we are Alawite and are not recognised by either the Shia or Sunni. We are different, we have to admit."

He paused for a moment, sighing deeply and went on. "Don't forget that we are a minority. I wish I could have stepped down at the beginning and –" the president stopped talking suddenly as a Syrian official approached.

"I grieve over the loss of your great mother. It is really a tragic event, Mr President. Lady Anissa was a mother for all Syrians. Her death is a great loss for the country and the Arabic nation! I am so sorry, sir," the Member of the Public Assembly said.

"Thank you! Mohammed," Bashar al-Assad said.

Sheik Ahmed Hasson gave a short speech talking about 'the great Arabic lady'. He wept whilst praising the President's mother and talking about her role. "She was really a great woman. She stood by her husband, our great leader, the martyr, Hafiz al-Assad, in very difficult times. She was a strong support for her son as well, Mr President, in ruling the country. Ultimately, we are all here to say with great sadness and sorrow: 'Goodbye mother. Goodbye to the greatest woman on the planet. Even though you left our world, you will stay alive in our hearts. God, bless you, Lady Anissa, Allah grant you the Paradise!'"

"Hypocrisy," Maher whispered in his brother's ear as Hasson had left. "They are all hypocrites. Crocodile tears. I don't trust them at all."

Bashar al-Assad nodded and commented, "I know! But we need those dogs. A dog that's barking with you is better than one barking against you. I enjoyed that speech. He is a good speaker."

Maher al-Assad grinned, "He's really a good dog."

Suddenly, the President whispered, "Look over there, Maher. Look at the entrance. The Russian Ambassador, Azamat Kulmuhametov, is here."

Bashar al-Assad rose from his chair and went over to welcome the guest. Maher also went to welcome the Ambassador.

"I grieve over the loss of your mother, Mr President. I also would like to convey the condolences of my leader, Vladimir Putin, to you and your family," the Ambassador said.

"That is very kind of both of you, sir." Bashar al-Assad said humbly and indicated towards an armchair. "Please take a seat Mr Kulmuhametov."

"Mr Putin is really a sincere friend of Syria. I appreciate his significant support," Bashar al-Assad said.

"The Russian leader never lets down his allies and friends."

The Ambassador smiled, continuing, "However, to be perfectly frank with you, Mr President, my leader isn't happy with the Iranian influence over your government. I think it's time to put an end to their interventions in the government."

"But you know we are all in this alliance and in the same trench against terrorism. Iran has always been the enemy of Islamic terrorist groups."

"I know." the Ambassador nodded, "You're right, sir, but we have different interests. We won't allow anybody to go beyond the limit."

Bashar al-Assad shrank a little, "Understood, Mr Ambassador."

After everybody had left, Bashar al-Assad became drained with exhaustion. He leant on a sofa and covered his eyes.

"Mr President. Mr President, wake up please," one of his guards said and added. "Sorry to disturb you, sir, but we have to leave this place."

"I'm so tired. Leave me alone. I am going to stay here overnight," he said.

"Please, Mr President, come with us for your safety, sir. Many people know that you're in the palace, sir. The palace is within missile range of the rebels."

For security reasons, the President had been forced to keep changing locations each night and was moving around between houses in central Damascus. He had rarely slept in the same bed for more than one night since the uprising had started in 2011.

As soon as Bashar al-Assad entered the newly arranged apartment, he slumped exhausted on the bed but thoughts attacked him from every side and stole the sleep from his eyes. *"I cannot understand what's going on around me. Why is my mind stuck? Everything has become upside down. I don't understand what the Russian Ambassador wants. He was talking nonsense. How can I reduce the Iranian's influence? They took control of everything once I lost most of my trustworthy officers in the war. This conflict had now entered a chaotic state and gone beyond anything anyone anticipated. I can't step down or leave. It's too late."*

Suddenly, his thoughts turned to the terrible image of Gaddafi crying and asking for mercy after being captured by Libyan rebels. He looked around while he put his hand on his neck. *"I don't want the same tragic end."* Then he murmured, *"I wish I'd never become President. I'm really finished."*

He remembered the Iranians as well. He had a sip of wine and popped two sleeping pills whilst talking to himself, "It's an unreasonable demand. Kicking my brother, Maher, out of his position will put me in difficult circumstances." He looked at his watch then returned to his thoughts. *"I don't care as long as Israel sticks to the promises made to my father and remains by my side. But my future seems to be in the hands of the Russians and the Iranians and I can't now refuse their demands. I will be the scapegoat if these governments* make a deal with the US and the European Union. *There is so much pressure by the European Union on the US to intervene to help them to stop the flow of migrants engulfing their countries. Meanwhile, the opposition groups are getting together too and are now ready to replace me. And the rebels are gaining new territory every day."*

He looked towards the window, seeing the first ray of light of a new day, and sighed with a heavy heart. *"I need a break. I definitely need a break."*

* * * * *

Eventually, a Greek vessel arrived and rescued the refugees, including Ali's group, taking them to the nearest island. It was a small, empty place. There was a large tent, which had been built by one of the human rights organisations to protect the refugees and give them help on their arrival. The tent was full of migrants who had come from other parts of Turkey.

"How long have you being here?" Ali asked one of them.

"Three days."

Ali frowned. "Three days in these terrible conditions?" Ali exclaimed, "It's a long time."

Essam hugged his children and kissed them whilst trying to stop his tears flowing, "Sorry, my children! I had no other options," then he sighed deeply. "Alhamdullilah. You're still alive," he gazed at his wife who was still in a state of shock and wasn't talking. She burst into tears and finally said, "I can't believe that we are still alive."

"We were really lucky that my mobile was working."

"You were clever to put it inside that balloon," Wafa said.

He wiped his tears and nodded, "Sadly, thousands of Syrian people have died in similar conditions."

Ali al-Halabi and some other men opened boxes that were in the tent, looking for food.

"Biscuits and water in these boxes," Ali said.

Essam nodded, "That will be enough for the moment."

Ali read the label on the boxes and said, "One of the human rights organisations built this tent and left these boxes in case people arrive. They can survive for at least a few days."

Ali looked at his wife and asked, "Why is Nadir crying? What's wrong with him?"

"He's sick. His temperature is very high."

Ali strained, "What can I do? There's no doctor here."

"When are we going to leave this lifeless island?" Zineb asked with grief.

"Only Allah knows!"

"You should ask someone," she said.

"None of the people here know anything."

* * * * *

The killing machine in the cities of Syria was taking more lives every day. The fighting was going on in most parts of Syria. At the end of April 2016, the stronghold of rebel-held Aleppo was brutally attacked by Russian and Syrian air forces with missiles. The bombardment was very heavy, the smoke covered the sky and everything was prey to fire, leading to the destruction of many homes. Many buildings, including mosques and hospitals were razed to the ground, resulting in a large number of civilians being killed or wounded, most of them women and children. Meanwhile, a missile landed on the roof of Al Quds Children Hospital in al-Atarib. Dr Muhammad Waseem Maaz, the only paediatrician who had stayed on in Aleppo, was killed whilst carrying out his duties, along with at least twenty-seven fellow staff and patients. One could see trapped children and babies under the wreckage and their body parts were spread everywhere. Screaming and crying filled the air.

The international community turned away, as leaders of major countries including the US and the European Union chose to ignore the situation. They seemed to be waiting for the monsters to finish the job. The attack lasted for weeks and left part of the city completely devastated.

TV channels broadcasted the tragic attack on the Al Quds Children's Hospital. A father was crying from the depths of his heart whilst taking half of the body of his dead son out from under the rubble, leaving the other half under the wreckage. He cried and his tears flowed down his cheeks, his heart breaking, "Where are you Ban Ki-moon? Where are you Nabil Alarabi? Where are you Obama and where are your 'red lines'? What has this child done? Tell me, what? You're all criminals. He is not a terrorist. All of you have participated in killing my son. I will curse you to Allah. All of you are hypocrites."

His words echoed and were heard by everyone except the leaders of major countries, all of whom had the power to stop the monsters committing more crimes. One of the White Helmets workers screamed, "Help... help, I can hear a voice under the rubble. There's somebody here! Still alive."

Hospitals, schools, mosques and the White Helmets workers were being deliberately targeted by aircraft. More than ten White Helmets workers were killed in al-Atarib on the outskirts of Aleppo in separate incidents.

"Everybody must lie down, quickly. There's aircraft approaching!" somebody shouted.

But before he had finished his words, a Russian aircraft fired its missiles causing more devastation and chaos. People were running here and there in terror as death rained down upon them.

* * * * *

It was a new beautiful day and the sun appeared over the horizon. Zineb looked towards her husband and said, "Two days have passed now and nobody's bothered to give us any attention. Even though the Greek authorities know that we are here without food and water."

"You're right Zineb. The problem is that we are running out of food and water. We've only got enough biscuits and water for today."

Before the sun set, a Greek ship arrived at the island to take the refugees to mainland Greece.

A few days later, Essam, along with some of the other refugees and their family, continued their journey towards the European Union, the 'dream land'. In Macedonia and Hungary, Essam and his family were inhumanely treated while making their way to Germany. They, along with several hundred refugees, were forced to camp in a muddy field on Hungary's border with Serbia, awaiting permission to cross or be transferred to a reception refugee centre in another part of the country. The refugees were surrounded by Hungarian policemen, and forced to sleep in extremely cold weather in the open air. One could see mothers and fathers, utterly miserable, trying to protect their babies and children from falling victim to the cold.

In a Greek village near the border with Macedonia, around a thousand refugees found a break in a fence after walking for hours through a river, ignoring heavy rain and the extremely cold weather of the winter of 2016. Frantically, the refugees crossed fast-flowing water whilst carrying their children and belongings on their shoulders and heads.

Eventually, Essam and his family reached Germany. It was a tortuous journey with lots of unpleasant adventures and full of fear and almost unbearable humiliation. All Syrian migrants had a story to tell. Essam and his family had left behind their homeland, their relatives, their hopes and dreams as well as their belongings and property. They had been forced to leave their home and their country after the Moscow monster's air forces had destroyed their town.

The German authorities were kind to the refugees and many Germans welcomed them at the border. The German Interior Minister, Hans-Peter Friedrich, greeted the refugees. The first Syrian refugees were granted temporary asylum in Germany. On the other hand, German racists groups were totally against their own government as regards the refugee issue. A 'national front' movement made several demonstrations whilst others attacked some of refugees and set their tents on fire as a protest against the government's policy. Essam's family and hundreds of other refugees felt fearful, being attacked by those groups. Days later, the first refugee camp that had been set by the government was destroyed by mobs.

"If I had known this would happen to us, I wouldn't have come here," Essam murmured sadly.

Essam's wife sighed from the depths of her heart as she looked at the baby in her lap, then burst into tears, "It looks like death is following us. We fled the Syrian regime's hell to the European racism's fire."

Ali al-Halabi and his family decided to postpone their journey towards Germany as their son, Nadir, was still ill.

Chapter Fourteen

It was a lovely sunny day in the spring of 2016. A Turkish vessel was sailing towards the coast of Turkey having come from Greece. It was carrying hundreds of refugees and migrants against their will. According to the agreement Turkey had recently signed with the European Union, all migrants who had come from Turkey would be returned to it. Dikili, a small coastal town in Izmir province, received the first wave of migrants who had been sent back from European Union countries. The town's inhabitants protested, not far from the port, against the returnees. The refugees weren't happy to be sent back to Turkey even though the journey was safer, shorter and more comfortable under the supervision of Turkish coastguards and security forces. The TV correspondents and journalists were also in their company. But the refugees were more nervous, depressed and unhappy. The dreams of a better life in 'dream land' had been shattered. The money spent reaching their goal was lost. Everyone had his own story of misery and his own personal tale of what had driven him to leave his country.

Human rights groups and the UNHCR had condemned the EU-Turkey deal as immoral, calling it, 'an historic blow to human rights'. Most of the returnees were from Pakistan and Bangladesh along with the Syrians, who had no documents. As soon as the returnees arrived on Turkish soil, they were greeted by immigration officials waiting in a temporary tent in the port of Dikili, preparing to interview and interrogate them.

Ali al-Halabi and his family were among the returnees.

* * * * *

In mid-July 2016, a coup attempt carried out by a faction of the Turkish army struck against Erdogan's government in Turkey. The Army seized airports and bridges across the country and controlled squares and streets in Izmir and Istanbul in particular. The President had been attacked by helicopters and aircraft at his holiday residence at the Marmaris Hotel in Turkey. A few hours later Erdogan arrived at Istanbul International Airport after announcing, on a private TV channel, using his mobile phone, that he was still alive and leading the country, and requesting Turkish people go out in the streets and protect their government and the democracy. Thousands of people answered swiftly. They went out and filled the streets and squares in the major cities and towns and were able to ruin the coup. The attempted coup shuffled the cards in Turkey and affected its relationship with the western countries including the US. The Turkish government accused Muhammet Fathullah Gulen, living in exile in the United States, of plotting in the failing coup and an Istanbul court issued an arrest warrant against him. The attempted coup also had a negative impact on the Syrian revolution. Only Russia stood against the coup attempt despite its differences with Erdogan. The Turkish role in

Syria shrank whilst Russia intensified its aggression in Aleppo.

Vladimir Putin sent his only aircraft carrier to Syria. He had lost patience with the battle for Aleppo and now Iran was also sending more ground troops to take back the eastern part of the city, which was still in the hands of the rebels, at whatever cost. Russian air raids intensified by the hour, pouring its hellish bombs upon Aleppo, destroying schools, houses and hospitals, using all weapons at their disposal, including weapons of mass destruction such as chemicals, cluster bombs and phosphoric bombs.

There were a large number of casualties each day on the soil of Aleppo in particular. One could hear children screaming and see parts of human bodies spread in the flames.

* * * * *

In a temporary accommodation, in Nizap refugee camp in Turkey, near the Syrian border, Zineb was cooking when her husband's mobile rang.

"Ali. Your mobile is ringing. This is the second time," Zineb said.

Ali picked up his mobile and listened carefully and said with grief, "Oh my God. When did this happen?"

"A few hours ago," The person at the other end of the phone replied.

"I will be with you as soon as possible. Please wait for me."

He hung up and put his hand on his head trying to control his tears, "Another atrocity," he murmured.

"Why you're crying Ali? What's the problem? Tell me what's wrong? What's the problem?" Zineb asked with surprise.

He looked at her with sadness, "His wishes came true. We lost a hero. We really lost him."

"Who are you talking about Ali? You drive me mad."

"I grieve over the loss of your father, Zineb. That's his fate."

"What!" she yelled.

"Sadly, your father, Zineb, has been chosen by Allah as a martyr. He was killed in the way he wanted."

She burst into tears and couldn't utter a word. She cried and cried, nonstop.

"He was killed in a Russian air raid on Aleppo. He was such a brave man, Zineb. Don't cry, darling, please."

He placed his hand on her shoulder gently and said, "I have to go to his burial. I have to attend the funeral."

"What are you saying! Are you mad, Ali?" she cried and could hardly control her crying, saying, "I will not let you go. You want to leave us here in Turkey alone? I don't want to lose you as well."

"I have to fulfil my promise, Zineb," Ali said with grief.

Then, he paused for a moment and wiped his tears, remembering the time when he made a promise to his uncle, Omar al-Halabi. He told Zineb, "One night we were stopped by a military vehicle nearby one of the regime's checkpoints. The soldiers insisted on taking me with them. Your father pretended to leave and then all of a sudden opened fire with his rifle, killing all of them. There were four of them. He was slightly wounded in the arm. He smiled at me, whilst I tightened up his wound with a piece of cloth, and said, 'Promise me that when I die, you bury me with your own hands, son.'

I smiled back. And I asked him, "How about if I die before you uncle?"

He replied angrily, "Don't say that Ali!"

Zineb looked at her husband, tears rolling down her cheeks and said, "I don't know when this killing will stop. When it will come to an end? Why do the monsters of Russia and Iran insist on destroying our country, killing us and our children?"

"Russia and Iran couldn't do this dirty job without the international community's approval or at least their silent agreement," he said.

She kept crying.

"It's an unbelievable conspiracy. Allah alone is able to stop it," he added.

Ali continued, "Anyway, Zineb, I have to be there as soon as possible."

"Promise me that you will come back," Zineb cried.

"I do promise, my love."

"But, how you will get there?" she asked.

"Don't worry about me, darling. I can manage."

"I will call my friend, Tariq, to get me to the border."

They hugged each other and cried goodbye.

Half an hour later, Ali set off in Tariq's car. When they reached the border, he said, "Please, Tariq, look after my wife and son. I have a feeling that I won't return."

"Why put your life at risk then?" Tariq asked.

"I don't know. I have to go. There is an irresistible power driving me there. Who knows what my destiny may be," Ali said, just managing to control his tears.

Tariq nodded, "Take care of yourself Ali. Your family is in safe hands."

Meanwhile, the attack on Aleppo was intensifying. Russian forces rained down on Aleppo hundreds of missiles and the regime showered the area controlled by rebels in the city with barrel-bombs whilst Iran brought more fighters to raid it.

Ali al-Halabi crossed the border with the help of a smuggler. He was surprised to find Samir Masood awaiting on the Syrian side. They hugged each other. The car set off towards Aleppo. Ali was astonished when he saw the extent of the latest destruction caused by the missiles and air barrels dropped by the Syrian regime. He managed to control his tears as he passed by al-Atarib and he frowned, "I cannot believe my eyes. There is so much more devastation in the city, Sam —."

"Watch out Samir!" Ali shouted suddenly.

A missile landed very close to the car.

"For days, the enemy missiles haven't stopped for a moment. Unfortunately, it's caused lots of casualties," Samir said.

"It looks like Russia wants to destroy the city and bring it down on top of its inhabitants."

Samir nodded, "Ali, we are approaching. We have to be more cautious."

Ali frowned. "Now I understood what, Major Hider Nizar meant when he told me that the rebels had been fooled by the major countries who would not let this regime fall. I didn't believe him at that time but he was absolutely right."

"Watch out there's aircraft firing its missiles at us, try to take…"

Before Ali could finish his speech, a missile hit the car directly.

Epilogue

Death was flying over the heads of the Syrians, appearing not to want to leave the Syrian sky for even a moment. It was in every corner, in every street and in every place, over the entire country. People fleeing from the killing were more likely to meet it at hospitals, schools and mosques. One could see dead bodies, body parts and blood under the rubble of houses, under the wreckage of mosques and elsewhere. Ultimately, the horrific killing machine of the regime and its allies were claiming soul after soul without pause. The killers were, clearly, showing no mercy and making no distinction between men, women and children. It appeared that everyone opposing Bashar al-Assad was required to die. The highest rates of victims were children, women and the elderly. Nobody was safe in the Republic of Horror, whilst the 'Dracula' of Damascus and his allies turned the country into hell. They appeared to relish the bloodshed, killing and the spreading of fear. One could see children and women running in every direction, screaming in hysterical states of horror, during each attack or raids, looking for shelter to avoid the hail of bombs and missiles.

The Syria crisis had become a moral crisis and a humanitarian disaster. Shi'ite militias, led by Iran, alongside the forces of Bashar al-Assad were using the superiority of the Russian Airforce and missiles to commit genocide and war crimes. In Aleppo, the regime displaced the Syrian people who had lived in that city for four thousand years, with the intention of changing the demographic population in the major cities and reducing the dominance of the Sunni population.

There were also thousands of Syrians dying in the darkness of the jails in horrible circumstances by different methods. In February 2017, Amnesty unveiled an alarming report about the killing carried out by the regime in Saydnaya prison, one of most infamous prisons in Syria. The report stated that thirteen thousand opponents of Bashar al-Assad were secretly hanged in the jail, according to witness statements by four former guards who had worked at the prison. The bodies were dumped in two mass graves on the outskirts of Damascus on military land in Nahja and Qatana. Thousands of others had died from torture and starvation in the prisons as well as other jails in the entire country, including Palmyra and Mezza.

At the beginning of April 2017 another horrific chemical weapons attack occurred in Idleb province, Khan Sheikhun. The Syrian regime backed by the Russian Airforce raided the area, again using Sarin gas. The attack resulted in many more civilian deaths and injuries, including children. The attack reminded us of the brutal chemical weapons attack carried out by Bashar al-Assad's forces in Ghouta in 2013, almost four years previously, killing hundreds of people, most of them children. The regime escaped punishment at that time and ignored the Chemical Weapons Convention and the America 'red lines' drawn by the then President, Barack Obama.

The tragic story continues despite the fact that Bashar al-Assad's regime, which controls less than half the country, has gained the upper hand in the conflict as a result of a global conflict of interests. The Syrian people continue to pay the heaviest price. It is an unforgivable crime that the people of Syria, particularly children and women, are being killed by missiles, bombs and chemical weapons in such a dreadful way and that the leaders of the world's conscience are not revolted enough to stop the aggression and destruction.